Mystery Motive

Superintendent Folly Mysteries
by John Creasey

The Gallows Are Waiting
Close the Door on Murder
First a Murder
Mystery Motive

Mystery Motive

John Creasey

David McKay Company, Inc.
Ives Washburn, Inc.
New York

MYSTERY MOTIVE

COPYRIGHT © 1947, 1973 BY JOHN CREASEY

Originally published under John Creasey's pen name of Jeremy York

First American Edition, 1974

LIBRARY OF CONGRESS CATALOG CARD NUMBER: 74-83456
ISBN 0-679-50486-9

MANUFACTURED IN THE UNITED STATES OF AMERICA

Mystery Motive

CHAPTER ONE

OFFICIAL VISIT

Two policemen turned into the short drive. Jim Gantry saw them from his study window, and immediately lost his train of thought. Angela, his wife, saw them from the bedroom below the study, and became suddenly conscious of her untidy hair. Their son and heir, baptised Mark Alan but generally called Tub, saw them from the side door, where he was playing with a ball of wool he had discovered, with the delight of two-year-olds, on the table in the sitting-room.

Only Tub took action.

Seeing the two tall men in bright-buttoned uniforms, the ball of wool lost its allure. It dropped unheeded as he ran towards them.

Two yards away, Tub stopped and stared. He was a cautious child, and looked to the other side to make the first advance. The taller of the two policemen smiled genially.

'Hallo, young man.'

Tub put his thumb to his mouth.

'You'll catch it,' said the shorter policeman, who, rather plump, was perspiring gently under the warmth of the morning sun. It was early May, and the old garden was bright with new life, the long stretch of lawn fresh and green. 'Is your daddy in?'

'Daddy!' cried Tub, delighted at hearing a word that he recognised. 'Daddy!' he repeated, pointing to the study window where his father, Jim Gantry, was looking down. The taller policeman, who was younger than his companion by at least ten years, glanced up and smiled. 'Daddy!' called Tub, and went running towards the house, followed more sedately by the visitors.

Upstairs, Jim and Angela met on the first-floor landing,

7

Angela having meanwhile arranged her hair becomingly beneath a twisted scarf of bright green.

'How do you know they want to see *you*?' Jim inquired teasingly.

'Well, someone's got to open the door. Paddy's shopping.'

'Then let us go together,' said Jim, putting his arm about her shoulders and kissing her ear. 'Darling, I love you,' he said, and laughed when she whispered: 'Hush, they might hear!' 'Let the whole world hear,' he answered, 'the police included, a spot of romance will brighten their dull lives.'

They walked down the stairs side by side, Jim Gantry rather above medium height, dark-haired, not particularly good-looking but with eyes which usually held a smile. Angela, half a head shorter, with a few strands of auburn hair escaping from the scarf and curling against her happy face.

First, Tub came in sight. Angela saw the tangled wool, and exclaimed: 'Tub!'

'Ahhh!' scolded Tub, pointing accusingly at the wool. 'Ahhh!' The first sound was undoubtedly meant for the wool alone, the second was rather more hesitant, as if he wondered whether or not his mother would blame the wool and let him go scot-free.

The taller policeman was standing with the ball in his hands, winding industriously. His companion stood beside him, frowning as if he thought that such things should be left to the parents.

'Good morning,' said the younger man. 'Are you Mr. and Mrs. Gantry?'

'That's right,' said Jim. 'Master Gantry has already introduced himself, I gather.'

'Very thoroughly,' smiled the other. 'I wonder if you can spare me a few minutes? I am Detective-Sergeant Cunningham, this is Police-Officer Small.'

'How are you?' asked Jim absently. 'Yes, come in. Do you want to see one or both of us?'

'I would rather see you both,' said Sergeant Cunningham.

Jim led the way into the sitting-room, followed by his wife. She was as puzzled as he was, and neither of them had any idea why policemen should want to see them.

Jim indicated chairs and offered cigarettes.

8

'I won't smoke now, thanks,' said Cunningham, as he sat down in a chair near the window. A shaft of sunlight caught his face. He was remarkably good-looking, pleasantly tanned, with bright, smiling blue eyes. He looked quite at home, but Small sat uncomfortably on the edge of an upright chair.

Cunningham spoke with a note of gravity in his voice.

'I wanted a word with you first, because I'm afraid I am going to give you rather a shock.' A reassuring smile lit up his face as he saw the anxiety in Angela's eyes. 'I understand you employ a man named O'Hara.'

'Paddy!' exclaimed Angela.

Jim looked thoughtfully at the sergeant.

'Yes,' he said. 'O'Hara works here.'

'What on earth has Paddy been doing?' demanded Angela.

Cunningham shook his head.

'I'm afraid he's been doing what he shouldn't. We are investigating a number of local burglaries, and have reason to believe that O'Hara is concerned in them.'

'How ridiculous!' exclaimed Angela. 'Paddy is as honest as the day!'

A change came over Cunningham. He was now as official as Small, although more composed and self-confident.

'I hope you are right, Mrs. Gantry. But we have information which makes it necessary for us to question him, and I shall be greatly obliged if you will let us search his room.'

'But this is absurd!' declared Angela.

Jim sent her a quick smile.

'I don't think the police would come along if they hadn't some grounds for suspicion,' he said, lightly. He looked at Cunningham. 'I agree with my wife though. We would trust Paddy anywhere and with anything, but that doesn't mean that you can't search his room. I would like to be there when you do it, of course.'

'Yes, that's all right,' said Cunningham.

Small stirred, but did not voice a protest.

'Hang it, Jim, you're as bad as they are,' accused Angela. 'It isn't fair to allow them to search Paddy's room when his back's turned. Why don't you wait until he returns and speak to him himself? That would be a much fairer way of doing things.'

Cunningham smiled. 'I assure you that we won't do anything without telling O'Hara, Mrs. Gantry. Everyone has his rights, you know. He will be given legal assistance if he can't afford to pay for it himself.'

'It will never get as far as that!'

'Which brings us to the question: just how far has this gone, Sergeant?' Jim spoke quietly, and Cunningham looked at him with new respect. Mrs. Gantry's reactions were understandable enough; her husband's were much cooler and more reasonable.

'Can't you wait until he's back?' demanded Angela. 'He's only gone up to the shops.'

'He's been gone longer than we expected,' Jim said.

'I'm afraid that is our fault,' murmured Cunningham. 'He was taken into the police station for questioning.'

'So it's gone as far as that,' said Jim.

'Do you mean you've charged him with *burglary*?' demanded Angela.

'I think it likely that he will be charged before the day is out,' said Cunningham. 'Whether or not we find anything in his room will have something to do with that, of course. I am really sorry that I've had to worry you, and it's very good of you to be so helpful. Will you take me to his room?'

Jim got up and ushered the two policemen into the hall. Then turning back to Angela, he murmured:

'Look here, darling, we know this is all a lot of nonsense and that Paddy will be cleared, but we mustn't put their backs up, you know. I've no doubt they have a search-warrant. Cunningham's behaved very nicely, and we might want his help for Paddy before it's over. Be friendly towards him.'

'Friendly!'

'Well, I shall know what they find *if* they find anything,' said Jim. 'It wouldn't be a bad idea if you made a cup of tea to offer them when they come down.' He squeezed her hand and hurried out into the hall. 'Sorry,' he apologised. 'I'll lead the way.'

It was an old, rambling house, much too large for the Gantrys, although it had advantages. Jim had been able to take over the whole of the top floor for his work and his papers, where, except for one room which was Paddy's, he had a study and two small offices.

The first flight of stairs was wide and imposing; the second narrow and uncarpeted. Boards creaked as the three men walked up. The second-floor landing was also uncarpeted and there was no furniture; it looked uninhabited. The study, the door of which was standing open, quickly dispelled that impression. In the window was Jim's large, flat-topped desk and round the walls were well-filled bookcases. A carpet stretched from wall to wall.

Passing the room, they turned to a closed door, which Jim opened. Paddy's bedroom was at the back of the house, and looked on to a big, orderly, attractive garden. Beyond it were the roofs of the houses in the next street, mostly hidden by tall trees.

'You've a lovely spot here,' remarked Cunningham.

'Yes,' said Jim. 'We were lucky. I think I was the last person in Malling to find an unfurnished house to rent!'

It was a large room with sloping ceilings, two wide windows with ledges on which photographs and ornaments stood. None of the furniture was good, but the room looked pleasant and was tidy and clean.

Cunningham took a swift look round. Small's glance took longer, seeming to ponder over every detail.

'Where do you start?' asked Jim.

'I'll try the dressing-table,' Cunningham said. 'You look in the cupboard, Small, will you?'

They set to work. Jim sat in one of the easy-chairs and watched them, but his mind was not entirely with them. He kept thinking of Angela's indignation. Cunningham was twice as quick as his companion. He emptied the dressing-table drawers and looked through the contents, unfolding handkerchiefs and ties, which he refolded with scrupulous precision before replacing. Small lifted out Paddy's few clothes. His best suit, of rather a bright blue, his Melton overcoat, his shabby raincoat and a dressing-gown of startling pattern. Paddy had obtained that dressing-gown only a few weeks earlier. He had displayed it with great pride and to the accompaniment of admiring comments from Angela and Jim.

Small left it on the bed, but put back everything else after going through the pockets. Then he took out three pairs of boots. Feeling inside each one, he found nothing, put them

11

back and then came out with another pair. Small paid them special attention, and left them by the side of the bed.

Cunningham was also putting things on the bed. A pair of royal blue pyjamas, another recent acquisition; several shirts, some cuff-links. Jim began to feel the stirring of alarm. The methodical way in which the policemen worked, their way of picking out certain things and putting them aside without comment or hesitation, worried him. Soon, the pile on the bed reached formidable proportions. Cunningham had finished the dressing-table and was working on a chest of drawers. From one drawer he took a pigskin wallet and Jim saw his eyes glint. He examined the wallet closely, looking into every partition; it seemed to be empty, but he put it aside and then took the lining paper out of the same drawer. He seemed disappointed as he replaced the paper and closed the drawer. For a moment he stood looking round. Then Small, still busy in the built-in wardrobe, came out, red-faced, holding a small attaché case.

'It's locked,' he said.

'Let me have a look at it,' said Cunningham. He brought out a bunch of keys from his pocket. He tried at least half a dozen without result, but at last found one that fitted. The lid sprang back. Jim craned forward to look inside. There was a bundle of one-pound notes, forty or fifty in all. He wondered how Paddy could ever have saved so much money, for he was a spendthrift, with the most generous heart in the world.

Cunningham looked up.

'I'm afraid we'll have to give Mrs. Gantry bad news,' he said. 'Most if not all of this stuff has been stolen. Didn't it ever occur to you, Mr. Gantry, that O'Hara was adding to his wardrobe at a surprisingly fast rate?'

CHAPTER TWO

BAD NEWS

Cunningham spoke quietly, but his question jolted Jim. For a moment he looked at the pile on the bed without speaking. There were inferences in that question, and one was most evident; Cunningham was implying that he must have known that Paddy had no right to the things on the bed.

'No,' he said, at last.

'I don't quite understand you.'

'Do you know Paddy?' asked Jim.

'I have met him only once,' said Cunningham.

Jim laughed. 'Then you know he's a colourful fellow!' And —although I say it myself—I pay him pretty well. He's invaluable; literally a man-of-all-work. We can trust him to put Tub to bed if we want to go out early in the evening. He does all the garden and most of the cooking, and he's twice as successful at shopping as my wife. So he gets double the normal wage and his keep. We try to make him save, but half a crown a week is his limit, I think. The rest he spends as he earns— and more, because he indulges in a little flutter now and again, and he's the luckiest backer I've ever met. So, such additions to his wardrobe didn't strike me as being particularly odd.'

Cunningham took out the bundle of notes.

'He didn't buy these.'

'The notes themselves don't surprise me,' said Jim. 'He's sometimes won as much as thirty or forty pounds at a go. The fact that he locked it away is a little out of character.'

'I see,' said Cunningham. It was impossible to judge whether he believed Gantry or not. 'Have you seen this case before?'

'No.'

'Or the pigskin wallet?'

13

'No.'

'What about the other things on the bed?'

'As far as I can tell you, he has shown each one to me or to my wife,' said Jim. 'If they were stolen—perhaps I ought to say if he *knew* they were stolen—I can't imagine that he would have made such a display of them.'

'Perhaps not,' conceded Cunningham, 'although if he knew you had no suspicions he might have felt safe enough. All of the things on the bed are stolen goods, Mr. Gantry.'

'Well, I've got to take your word for that.'

'Thanks,' said Cunningham drily. 'Do you think you or your wife could say when these things were first brought into the house?'

'We could probably help with some of them, but not all,' said Jim. 'Paddy has worked for us for nearly twelve months. I know exactly when the dressing-gown arrived. It was two days after Easter. We had been away for the weekend and came back on the Wednesday and he showed it to us the same night.'

Small was making notes.

Cunningham said: 'Do you think Mrs. Gantry——'

'*Daddy!*' cried Tub. '*Daddy!*' Jim opened the door. Tub came tumbling in at a great pace, and Angela appeared behind him, carrying a tea-tray. Jim hid a smile.

'We usually have tea about eleven o'clock,' she said. 'I thought you might like a cup.' She put the tray on the chest of drawers, and then saw the clothes on the bed. Her smile disappeared. 'What on earth are they?'

'Exhibits to be used in evidence against Paddy,' Jim told her, 'or else against the man who sold them to Paddy, which is a different kettle of fish. Bless you, darling. I was dying for a cup of tea, and I expect our visitors were too.' He jumped up, while Angela stared in bewilderment at the 'exhibits', and Tub, attracted by the colours, pulled the dressing-gown from the bed. 'Mind you don't leave your fingerprints, Tub,' Jim warned him. 'That might land you in jail for goodness knows how long!'

Cunningham smiled rather tensely. 'You know this is a serious matter, Mr. Gantry, don't you?'

Jim finished pouring out a cup of tea, handed it to him, and said carefully:

'Yes. Serious for Paddy and possibly serious for me. Let me make two things clear. First, neither my wife nor I had any idea that any of these things were stolen. Second, both my wife and I are convinced that Paddy bought them in good faith.'

'My husband speaks for us both,' declared Angela. 'No, Tub, don't take the sash out! You'd better come downstairs with me.'

Tub looked rebellious, and seized a pair of tartan socks.

'Go with Mummy, old chap,' said Jim. 'Goodbye!' He waved at Tub who waved vigorously back, and the door closed sharply.

'You could hardly make yourself clearer,' said Cunningham.

Jim smiled. 'That's fine. I was anxious that there should be no misunderstandings. I suppose you want to take these things away with you.'

'Yes.'

'Well, I can't object to that, although I'll be glad if you will make a list of them and leave me a copy,' Jim said. 'And you'll have to count the notes, won't you?'

There were forty-one pound notes and three ten-shilling notes in the bundle. Cunningham and Small counted and checked, Jim refused an invitation to check them again, and watched Small make an inventory of the goods. When that was finished and the receipt signed, Cunningham said:

'Now I wonder if you will tell me what you know about O'Hara, Mr. Gantry.'

'Certainly. He came to us out of the blue, last July, when we were desperately in need of a man for the garden,' said Jim. 'He had no references but said he had been in the Army. He had lost his papers, which was understandable enough——'

Cunningham raised his eyebrows. 'Was it?'

'Well, yes. I thought it a little odd at the time, but once I got to know Paddy I saw that there was nothing surprising in it. He is the most careless fellow imaginable. But he's a good chap, you know. I don't rule out the possibility that he has let himself be influenced by someone else, but I think it's unlikely, and I believe the case will collapse.'

'Not on this evidence, I'm afraid,' said Cunningham.

'We'll see. Is there anything else you want to know about him? I've already given you an outline of his activities, and

15

my opinion of him.'

'Does he ever go out at night, to your knowledge?'

'If you mean in the evenings, he's out two or three times a week. Usually at the Crown, in the High Street.'

'I mean during the night,' said Cunningham.

'No. I've never heard him go out, and he's always up at half-past six or seven in the morning, bright-eyed and cheerful.'

'You mean, that if he has gone out at night after midnight —it has always been without your knowledge.'

'Yes.'

Small said: 'Do you mean to say anyone walking down those stairs wouldn't wake you up?'

Jim smiled serenely at the constable, and said gently: 'No, I don't mean that. I think I should have woken up had Paddy walked down the stairs. I'm quite sure that my wife would have done so as she is a very light sleeper. So if Paddy went out, it must have been by the window. You can probably tell if that's been used regularly. There's a porch just below, which he could reach quite easily.' Jim went to the window, opened it and pointed downwards. 'It could be done, I've no doubt, but I don't think it has been.'

'I see,' said Cunningham. 'Did you notice anything unusual about him this morning?'

'No, I can't say that I did. He was a bit later than usual.'

'How much later?' Cunningham asked, sharply.

'He didn't bring us tea until a quarter to eight. It's usually nearer seven. Tub was late waking up this morning, too, and that gave me a bad start in the day's work.'

'I'm sorry that we've had to delay you further,' said Cunningham, perfunctorily. 'Why do you think O'Hara was later this morning?'

'Presumably he overslept.'

'And that's not a habit of his?'

'No. But the chap's not a machine. Why the particular interest in this morning, Sergeant?'

'There was another burglary during the night,' Cunningham told him, while Small coughed and looked very portentous.

Jim wondered if there were anything more behind the interest in the previous night than Cunningham had admitted. He thought it wiser not to press the matter, however. Cunningham asked several more questions. Had they all slept soundly through the night? Had there been any noises to suggest that O'Hara had been about? Had he given any hint, during the morning, that he was more tired than usual?

To all of these questions, Jim replied 'No.'

'Well, I needn't worry you any more now,' said Cunningham. 'You've been very good, Mr. Gantry. I'm sorry that I had to spring this on you.'

'Well, it has certainly been rather a shock. Will Paddy be charged when you get back to the station?'

'That's not my province,' said Cunningham, cautiously. 'It will be up to the Inspector.'

'I see. Now, what about Paddy's defence?'

'As I told Mrs. Gantry, he will be given legal aid, if——'

'Oh no,' said Jim. 'I'll supply the legal aid, if necessary. You may think I am showing a remarkable concern for Paddy O'Hara,' he added, 'but he's practically one of the family. He's made himself so. And I should hate to think that anything went wrong because the legal aid put at his disposal wasn't up to scratch. Perhaps I'd better come along with you,' he mused. 'I can call and see Andrew Dale on the way. Do you know Dale?'

'Yes, I know all the solicitors in the town,' Cunningham said. 'Aren't you a friend of Mr. Dale?'

'Yes.'

Cunningham said in a quiet voice: 'Mr. Gantry, this is not my business, but I know Mr. Dale and greatly respect him. I don't think he would accept the defence in this case except out of friendship towards you. In fact I doubt whether he will accept it even if you press him. I am going out of my way and asking for trouble, I know, but I think I would wait a little while before you approach Mr. Dale.'

Jim looked puzzled. 'Oh, I see. Well, can I see Paddy?'

'That's up to the Inspector,' replied Cunningham.

'Right. Well, I'll wait for you downstairs.'

Jim made his way to the kitchen, where Angela was peeling potatoes, and looking very glum. He leaned against the draining-board.

'Fond of Paddy, aren't you?' he said.

'Of course I am.'

17

'I think he's in serious trouble,' Jim observed.

'Oh, don't be silly,' said Angela. 'Of course he's in serious trouble, or the police wouldn't have come here. I can't believe that all those things he showed us were *stolen*, Jim.'

Jim said: 'Put down that potato peeler, sweet, and look at me.' He rarely spoke so firmly, and Angela obeyed with a start. She had lovely eyes, a clear grey-green, but now they looked worried. 'When I say serious I mean much more than serious,' Jim went on. 'I have a feeling that the police have not told us the whole truth. It's come so suddenly, too. Had it been just an inquiry about a series of burglaries, I think they would first have made tentative inquiries and come later with a search-warrant.'

Angela said slowly: 'What do you think has happened?'

'I don't know,' said Jim, 'but I'm going to find out. Don't be too surprised if I'm late for lunch.'

Jim found the two policemen waiting for him in the hall. Their car had been left a little further along Bligh Avenue, a wide street with rambling old houses on either side of the same type as the Gantrys'.

There had been two burglaries in this very Avenue, Jim remembered.

Cunningham drove in silence during the ten minutes it took to reach the High Street. Here busy crowds were thronging the pavements, overspilling to the road—as always happened on market day. It was a gay and colourful scene, and normally Jim would have enjoyed it. Today he could think only of the police station, and the single-fronted building which housed Dale, Coombs and Dale, Solicitors. It was Cunningham's advice about Andrew Dale that had prompted Jim to talk as he had to Angela; if Andy Dale hesitated about taking Paddy's defence, then something serious must have happened.

'Put me down here, will you?' he asked Cunningham. 'I think I'll have a word with Dale first.'

Cunningham drew into the kerb.

'Thanks,' said Jim, 'that's been a great help.'

He thought Cunningham looked at him oddly. He walked quickly away, feeling more alarmed than he cared about. As he neared the solicitor's office, he noticed that a small crowd was gathering outside. Hurrying his steps he saw that they were staring at the frosted glass of the window across which *Dale, Coombs and Dale* was printed in gold lettering.

He looked over the heads of the people and read a type-written notice on the door: *Closed until 2.30 p.m.* That was astonishing. He heard someone say: '*Terrible!*' in a hushed tone and, schooling his voice, he asked:

'What is terrible?'

'Why, poor Mr. Coombs,' said his informant, with the hushed pleasure of one about to impart shocking news. 'Murdered in his own bed!'

Murdered, thought Jim, blankly. So they want Paddy for murder!

CHAPTER THREE

THE INSPECTOR HAS A COLD

Detective-Sergeant Cunningham tapped on Chief Inspector Forrest's office door and waited until he heard a gruff: 'Come in.' As he entered, Forrest sneezed. His eyes were watering and his large, flabby face was pale. Twice again he sneezed into a damp handkerchief. 'Damn this cold!' he exclaimed. 'Sit down, man.'

'Thank you, sir.' Cunningham pulled up a chair from a vacant desk by the wall.

'Well, what have you found out?'

'I've had a most interesting interview, sir,' said Cunningham.

'Have you got any results, that's the point,' demanded Forrest hoarsely.

'Considerable results, sir,' Cunningham assured him. 'We found about one-tenth of the stolen goods in O'Hara's room, and——'

'So we've got him!' exclaimed Forrest.

'We've certainly got a lot of evidence against him,' Cunningham said cautiously. 'And we've found Mr. Coombs's wallet, and the missing money.'

For a moment Forrest appeared to forget his cold. He rubbed his hands together with obvious delight.

'Well, that's excellent, Cunningham, excellent! You had no trouble with the Gantry's, then.'

'Not trouble, exactly,' said Cunningham.

'What do you——' Forrest broke off in a paroxysm of coughing. Tears trickled down his face and dropped to the papers in front of him. 'I should be in bed,' he added, almost accusingly.

'I certainly think it would be wise, sir,' said Cunningham,

sympathetically. 'I thought you should have been off duty yesterday, with that cold.'

'I was perfectly all right yesterday,' snapped Forrest. He sat back, gasping. 'I don't know what to do. With Urquhart away and Massey already busy, I—*atchoo*!'

'I think one day in bed will probably see you fighting fit again, sir,' said Cunningham, 'and I can look after things for twenty-four hours. I can come and report to you this evening, any time you like.' He spoke mildly but was repressing a sense of great excitement. Forrest was obviously too sick to work; once he gave up, he might be off for a week. The Superintendent was away ill, the other Chief Inspector at Malling was working on a particularly involved case. If Forrest gave up, Cunningham would be the senior officer of the C.I.D. branch. True, the Chief Constable would probably send for an Inspector from another town in the county, but there would be a chance of working without Forrest constantly at his elbow, correcting him irritably and without cause, taking all the credit for what he did, and showing no inclination to recommend his promotion. That was like Forrest. Promotion at Malling was difficult to get; when it came, age was the reason rather than ability. Cunningham was not being conceited when he thought that he was the most able man, apart from Urquhart, Massey and Forrest, at the station, and he was by no means sure that Forrest was really more able.

'But how *can* I leave now?' demanded Forrest. 'The Chief Constable will be here at half-past twelve, and—*atchoo*!'

'He would probably appreciate your thoughtfulness if you left a message that you were afraid of passing on your cold,' said Cunningham.

'The man's frightened to death of catching anything,' gasped Forrest. 'I——'

It was no good. There was scarcely a sentence he could finish without a sneeze. Cunningham rang for the Chief Inspector's car, and then offered to drive him home.

'You'd better stay on the spot,' spluttered Forrest. 'Now don't forget, Cunningham, make complete records of——'

And off he went again.

For a few minutes after Forrest had gone Cunningham sat at the desk, smiling contentedly. Then his smile disappeared.

21

He had nothing to gloat about. The Coombs murder might be straightforward, in which case it would mean just an excess of monotonous routine work. If it proved complicated, then he would have no easy task to prove his ability.

The telephone rang.

'Hallo,' said Cunningham, briskly.

'There's a Mr. Gantry here, sir, who would like to see Chief Inspector Forrest,' said the operator.

'Oh,' said Cunningham. 'Hold on a moment.'

He could see no point in talking to Gantry again now, although it might be worth while to find out why he had come so quickly. Probably it was because he had learned of the murder. There were some curious things about Gantry which Cunningham had already noted. The best thing to do was to put him off; it would do no harm to keep him on edge for an hour or two, and might even do good.

'Hallo,' he said. 'Tell Mr. Gantry that Chief Inspector Forrest has been called away, but that the officer in charge of the O'Hara case will see him this afternoon at three o'clock.'

'Very good, sir.' The operator rang off.

Cunningham pondered over the Gantry's for a few seconds. They were a pleasant couple. He had liked them both, in spite of Angela Gantry's attitude. Gantry was rather a mystery man——

He rang for Small, determined to have a fully detailed report ready before Colonel Maitland appeared.

Colonel Maitland seldom favoured the Malling police station with a visit. Although Malling was the county town, Langham, the largest town in Malshire, was near the northern fringe, and Maitland lived there. He was not popular at Malling. Abrupt to a point of curtness, he too often gave the impression that he looked on the staff as a collection of country clods.

At half-past twelve to the minute, Maitland's car drew up outside the police station. Cunningham, looking out of the window, watched the tall erect figure of the Colonel climb out. Cunningham frowned, but went back to his desk. His heart was beating uncomfortably fast, for Maitland would probably

22

rebuke him for not sending a message reporting Forrest's collapse.

A red-faced constable tapped on the door and put his head into the room. 'The Old Man's coming up the stairs, Mark,' he hissed, and immediately withdrew. Cunningham bent studiously over the papers that strewed the desk. When the door opened he looked up with a start.

'Good morning, sir!'

' 'Morning,' said Maitland. 'Where is the Chief Inspector?'

'He's down with a frightful cold, sir. He was afraid of passing it on to you.'

'Oh,' said Maitland. 'That was considerate of him.' He pulled a chair up for himself and sat down, taking off his gloves. Cunningham had never before realised that he was so big and powerful, or noticed the penetrating brilliance of his grey eyes. He grew even more nervous. 'You're Detective-Sergeant Cunningham, aren't you?'

'Yes, sir.'

'Let me have your report.'

Cunningham picked up a typewritten page.

'Tell me about it, don't read it,' ordered Maitland.

'Very good, sir.' With a pang of regret that the meticulous method of his written report would not now be noted, Cunningham began to read.

Arnold Coombs, Justice of the Peace and senior partner in *Dale, Coombs and Dale*, Solicitors, had been murdered between one o'clock and seven o'clock that morning. At seven, his manservant had found him in bed with his head battered. The room had been rifled, and various things stolen, including Coombs's pigskin wallet and forty-odd pounds in notes. This money Coombs's niece had handed to her uncle in one-pound notes the previous evening; it was money her husband had borrowed and which she had come to repay. The niece had been with her uncle for about an hour, leaving his house in Marlborough Avenue a little before ten o'clock. After that, Coombs had read in his library until one o'clock. This time was established by his servant, who never went to bed until his master had retired.

All the indications at the solicitor's house were that burglary had been intended, and that Coombs had woken up, found

23

a man in his room, and been attacked.

'I don't necessarily accept that, sir,' went on Cunningham, momentarily forgetting that he was talking to the Chief Constable. 'But it certainly looks probable. We have had a series of minor burglaries over a long period—seven months and three days to be precise—and in each case access was gained at a first-floor window, leaving signs that a ladder had been placed against the wall of the house. The same signs were there last night. Inspector Forrest has always believed that the burglaries were the work of one man. I myself have compiled a list of all the missing articles.'

'Have you worked on these burglaries from the beginning?'

'I missed the first two, sir. The Chief Inspector took the investigations over himself and I assisted him.'

'I see,' said Maitland.

For a moment, so fleeting that Cunningham wondered if he were mistaken, a twinkle appeared in the Chief Constable's eye. The twinkle seemed to say that Maitland understood well enough what Cunningham really meant—that he himself had handled the series of burglaries but that all the reports had been credited to Forrest. Could he have been mistaken in Maitland?

'What progress have you made?' asked Maitland.

'In the burglaries, very little until five nights ago,' Cunningham told him. 'Then the man was seen. He worked too late and dawn was breaking as he climbed out of the window of a house in Carroll Road. He had to leave the ladder, but there were no prints and nothing to give away his identity. We now know, however, that he was a small man with red hair. That narrowed inquiries down a great deal, sir.'

'I suppose it did.'

'I have interviewed a dozen men with red hair,' Cunningham went on. 'The next on my list was a man named O'Hara. He is a manservant at a house in Bligh Avenue. A family named Gantry moved into the house eighteen months ago. They've had little to do with local affairs, although Gantry was friendly with Mr. Andrew Dale——'

'Coombs's junior partner?' asked Maitland.

'Yes, sir. Gantry is rather an unknown quantity. He is a writer of a kind. That is, he writes articles for highly specialised magazines. He also works on other people's manuscripts, I understand, and has written a biography or two. He seems to make a good thing out of it.'

Maitland nodded.

'O'Hara was engaged by him about a year ago,' went on Cunningham. 'Without references and without Gantry having any knowledge of his past, if what he tells me is right. The Gantrys, in fact, were most emphatic about their trust in O'Hara, even when I found a large number of the stolen goods in his room, including the wallet and money that was taken from Mr. Coombs's room last night.'

Cunningham paused, but Maitland's face remained expressionless.

'Of course, O'Hara has been detained,' went on Cunningham, feeling rather flat. 'The Gantrys say they are going to arrange his defence. That is, defence against a burglary charge, I did not tell them of the murder. Gantry now knows about it, however, and called to see the Inspector. I sent a message down telling him to come again this afternoon.'

'I see,' said Maitland. 'Do you think the Gantry's are concerned?'

Cunningham hesitated. 'I think they might be, sir.'

'Why?'

'Well, if their story is true, they employed O'Hara with surprising carelessness,' said Cunningham. 'On the other hand, they might have known that he was a professional burglar. They knew he had a great number of articles in his possession of the kind you wouldn't expect a man in O'Hara's position to have. They say he told them that he bought them out of the proceeds of racing bets, but I can't see a man like O'Hara buying a silk dressing-gown worth about twenty-five guineas. He gets a good wage, but I'm puzzled about the situation.'

'You mean that it's possible that the Gantrys planned O'Hara's burglaries, took most of the proceeds, left some to him and invented the betting successes to explain his more extravagant purchases?' asked Maitland.

'Exactly, sir.' The Chief *was* clever.

'I see. What does O'Hara say?'

'He denies ever being out at night.' A note of complacency crept into Cunningham's voice. 'He even denied being out last night, but he slipped up there, sir! He was seen by one of our men, returning to Bligh Avenue about half-past four. He was actually seen to turn into the gate. Our man followed him. He let himself in with a key. And the Gantrys rather reluctantly admitted that he was up later than usual this morning. I don't think there is much doubt that O'Hara was at Mr. Coombs's house at the time of the murder, sir.'

'Is your case strong enough to take to court?'

'To the magistrates' court, yes, sir. It's nothing like strong enough yet for the Assizes, of course.'

'No. All right, Cunningham. What are you doing in uniform, by the way?'

Cunningham flushed. 'It was thought advisable for me to visit the Gantrys in uniform, sir, and I haven't had time to change. The idea was that they would not expect a sergeant in uniform to go to see them about a murder. Er—it was meant to disarm them,' continued Cunningham, floundering. That had been Forrests' idea, confound him, but he could hardly say so.

'I should keep out of uniform during this case,' advised Maitland. 'Chief Inspector Massey will be in charge, you will work with him. I shall expect to be informed of progress day by day. I think you should keep an eye on the Gantrys.' Maitland stood up. 'Telephone me this evening, at nine o'clock.'

CHAPTER FOUR

CUNNINGHAM'S DELIGHT

When the door closed, Cunningham leaned back in his chair and beamed at the ceiling. Cheers, and again cheers! Massey was involved in a special job and so busy that Maitland had virtually given him, Cunningham, charge of the case. Nothing could be more satisfactory. Now he could really get cracking; he might even be able to select his own men, and there was just a chance that Maitland would let him bring Reg Owen in, from Linton. He and Reg, together on this case...

He stopped day-dreaming, and went down to see O'Hara.

Jim Gantry left the police station soon after getting the message from Cunningham, but he did not go far.

He wanted to see O'Hara and he badly wanted legal advice. He stopped at a telephone kiosk and rang up Andrew Dale, but Andrew was neither at the office nor at his home.

Jim left the telephone box, passing a short, plump man who had been waiting beside it.

'Sorry if I've kept you,' he said.

'That's all right.' The man gave a bright smile. 'I've been waiting for you, not the telephone.'

'Oh,' said Jim. 'Why?'

'Care for an early lunch?' asked the stranger. 'I've booked a table for two over at Ye Olde Shoppe!'

There was something infectious in his smile and likeable in his manner. Merry blue eyes and a wide mouth complete the picture.

'Ye Olde Shoppe' was in fact the Malling Restaurant, housed in a centuries-old building and renowned throughout the county. It was opposite the police station.

'What do you want to see me about?' asked Jim.

'O'Hara,' said the short man.

Jim reflected for a moment, and then nodded acceptance. 'Right.'

'I didn't think you'd disappoint me,' said the stranger, cheerfully. 'I like a man who can make up his mind.' He led the way into the restaurant, where a waitress showed them to a window seat.

'Good! We can keep an eye on the police station from here,' the other said. 'It's one up on the man who doesn't know what's going on.' He put a card in front of Jim, which read: *William Lecky, Daily Record, Fleet Street, E.C.4.* My credentials,' he added. 'Now you have to ask me how I come to be here so soon after the murder!'

'All right, what's the answer?' asked Jim.

'A good local correspondent, the 9.20 from Waterloo and the dearth of news,' answered Lecky, promptly. 'I heard about it just before nine o'clock and I live only a few minutes' walk from Waterloo, so here I am.'

A waitress took their order. The restaurant was already filling, although it was barely mid-day. Oak beams stretched dark against cream walls, and horse-brasses glittered. There was a note of quiet hustle about them, while people streamed past the low windows and traffic grew thicker.

Jim was summing up both Lecky's story and his manner. The man would, of course, want a 'story'. Jim could see no harm in giving him one, if it would enlist his help.

'Do you always report crime?' he asked.

'When there is any crime,' answered Lecky. 'If you mean, have I had plenty of experience on jobs like this, the answer is yes. Ten years of it. Worried about O'Hara?'

'I am, rather.'

'Hmm. What's Cunningham been saying to you?'

Jim laughed.

'Off the record,' declared Lecky.

That was good enough, Jim decided, and over soup and steak-and-kidney pie he told Lecky what had passed between him and Cunningham. Lecky listened intently. Jim was so absorbed in his story that he did not notice that he was being eyed with more than usual interest by many people who came into the restaurant. He had been turning the interview with

Cunningham over in his mind, and could not account for the disquiet it had left with him. It went deeper, even, than his concern for Paddy.

'And that's all,' he finished, at last. 'I went straight to the police station but was told to go back this afternoon. You don't know anyhing about the police down here, do you?'

'A little,' said Lecky. 'Our local correspondent is pretty spry. Cunningham is about the best they've got now that the Superintendent, whose name I forget, is away on sick leave. Forrest went home just before you called, sneezing all over the place. So they'll either bring someone in from outside or leave it to Cunningham. I think they'll bring someone else in. Colonel Maitland, the Chief Constable, isn't likely to leave it to a sergeant. He's by way of being a martinet, though sound enough. I've met him once or twice.' Lecky broke off, staring out of the window. 'Well, well!' he exclaimed. 'Talk of the Devil! Here he comes.' They watched Maitland getting out of his car.

'Is he fair?' asked Jim.

Lecky cocked an eyebrow.

'You've a lot to learn, Gantry,' he declared. 'The police are always fair. Everywhere. Don't be misled by little crooks bleating about police persecution. Rogues have to be persecuted. Everything that they find against O'Hara will be closely examined and if there's a flaw in it, it will be rejected. Even if the police were careless, the Public Prosecutor wouldn't be. Don't worry about that.'

'That's fine,' said Jim. 'I was a little worried.'

'You're *too* worried,' said Lecky. 'Why?'

Jim pondered. Lecky's shrewdness at once amused and alarmed him. Perhaps he had shown Cunningham some evidence of his deep disquiet. Now, too, he realised the reason for that disquiet; he had not seen it before because he had not wanted to.

Paddy might be guilty.

'I can't really explain,' he said. 'Cunningham managed to alarm me. He almost implied that I knew more about the stolen goods than I admitted.'

'Do you?' asked Lecky, lightly.

'No.'

29

'Then what have you got to worry about?' Lecky finished his pudding, and offered cigarettes. 'It's an interesting business, Gantry. I can see it from the outside, but you're too closely concerned to get the right perspective. To all appearances, they have their man. You, on the other hand, are convinced that O'Hara isn't the man. Your opinion leads to one obvious conclusion, doesn't it?'

'And what is that?'

'That O'Hara's been framed.'

Jim looked at him thoughtfully. 'Framed' had a sinister ring about it. He had not thought of it before, but now he saw that it was quite possible. Other things flashed through his mind. Paddy had bought the things somewhere——

Lecky said: 'Either O'Hara did the job or he's been framed. We've got to accept those alternatives. Looking at it coldly, I should say that the first thing is to find absolute proof that Paddy did put money on horses, and occasionally won. Have you got that proof?'

'No,' admitted Jim.

'Do you know who he betted with?'

'No, but he was always studying form.' Jim laughed. 'Neither my wife or I are gamblers. But Paddy won us over completely.'

'The kind who can get away with anything,' murmured Lecky.

'I suppose so.'

'Well, the first job is to find his bookie,' said Lecky. 'Then we've got to get the dates of these burglaries and find out whether they coincided with Paddy's flush periods.'

'Yes,' admitted Jim, 'but——'

'Let's leave the "buts" for a minute,' said Lecky, whose eyes had scarcely left the police station. 'The police will do exactly as I've suggested. If you show yourself as an interested party, it might be difficult for you. As a reporter I can go anywhere, and no questions asked—or hardly any. You leave it to me.'

'But why should you?' asked Jim.

'My dear chap, why shouldn't I?' replied Lecky, with his engaging grin. 'It's my job. The suggestion that reporters can show the police how to conduct a case is all my eye, of course, but sometimes we can get a different slant on it. And I can keep you abreast of police information. You are interested sufficiently to want that, aren't you?'

'Indeed I am.'

'Good! Now, this business of legal help. Why waste money? The police will provide it and the solicitor will only have to tell Paddy to keep his mouth shut. All that will happen will be a first hearing and probably an eight-day remand, followed by the inquest—they might even keep the first hearing until after the inquest. Then he'll come up again and be committed for trial at the Assizes. That can't come off for several weeks. I doubt if it will come in the Spring calendar, so you've plenty of time.'

'I don't want Paddy in jail awaiting trial indefinitely,' objected Jim.

'That isn't the point,' said Lecky. 'The point is that paying a man to come down from London, for instance, would be a waste of money because he can't do more than a local man could. What I'm trying to say is that our chances of proving that Paddy couldn't have killed Coombs won't be any slimmer, simply because we let a local man look after O'Hara for a start. Unless you've money to throw away, of course.'

'I haven't,' Jim told him, 'but lack of money isn't going to prevent Paddy having a first-class counsel.'

'Good! If it gets as far as a trial, you're right. We've got to stop it getting that far.'

Jim said: 'I still don't understand why you say "we".'

'I never could work outside a job properly,' confided Lecky, 'I like to take sides. And I prefer the lost cause! Hallo, here he comes. I'll be back.'

Lecky got up quickly and hurried out of the restaurant. Colonel Maitland was just leaving the police station. Lecky scurried across the road, dodging the traffic and forcing one driver to jam on his brakes. Maitland was about to enter his car as Lecky reached his side. Jim wished that he could hear what was being said. He fully expected Lecky to be sent about his business. Instead, Maitland was giving him a hearing...

'Is it true, sir, that you've sent for Scotland Yard assistance?' Lecky began, and Maitland looked at him in surprise. He also looked at the card which Lecky offered him, and the

31

faint twinkle, which Cunningham had noticed, appeared again.

'Not to my knowledge,' he said.

'Oh, good,' said Lecky. 'I always think it's better when the local police can get through on their own, sir, and I'm sure you do. Is O'Hara the man?'

'Aren't you a little hasty?' asked Maitland.

'I was wondering if it's all cut and dried,' declared Lecky, cheerfully. 'I don't want to waste my time in Malling if it's mere routine.'

'I doubt whether you would waste your time anywhere, Mr. Lecky,' said Maitland, drily. 'I am afraid I have no information for you. Detective-Sergeant Cunningham will doubtless spare you a few minutes later in the day. Good morning.'

Maitland got into his car and was driven off, while Lecky went back to the restaurant, paid the bill and accompanied Gantry back to the road.

'I gather that Maitland is giving Cunningham a run,' he said. 'That should be a help, because Cunningham is friendly with our local man. They haven't sent for the Yard, which means that they don't anticipate too much difficulty. You see, I get results!'

'You certainly do,' admitted Jim. 'Do you know of any way in which I can see O'Hara?'

'Ask Cunningham. He probably won't object. He might even like it if he thinks that you re mixed up in this. Now, can you give me a list of bookmakers in the town?'

'I'm afraid not,' said Jim.

'All right, I'll find 'em,' said Lecky. 'Can I look you up some time this afternoon? Or this evening?'

'Yes, any time'

They parted at a bus-stop, but at the last moment Jim decided not to go home at once. He waited until half-past two, when the office of *Dale, Coombs and Dale* was open, and then went in and asked for Andrew Dale.

'I believe he will be in soon, sir,' said a girl clerk. 'But only on urgent business.'

'My business *is* urgent,' said Jim, grimly.

'I see, sir. If you will wait in here——' She led the way to the waiting-room, and Jim settled down opposite a portrait of Arnold Coombs.

Coombs was a man whom he had met several times but never liked. The portrait depicted the narrow, thin face of an old man. The features were prominent, the forehead domed, the eyes hooded. Thin white hair was brushed back severely. In Jim's mind there came a picture of him lying in bed, with his head battered and that white hair stained red.

It was ludicrous to suppose that Paddy, short, wiry, forthright Paddy, whom Tub loved and who had so soon become part of the household, could be responsible for such a thing.

The door opened and Andrew Dale came in.

He looked very tired. Lean and good-looking, he stood by the door, smiling faintly; but his face was drawn.

'Hallo, Andrew. I'm so very sorry.'

'Thanks.'

There was no point in beating about the bush.

'You know they suspect Paddy, don't you?'

'They don't know Paddy.'

Jim's eyes lit up. 'Do you feel that way about it, too?'

'Of course I do,' said Andrew. 'But we needn't stay here, let's go into my office.'

It was a large, airy room on the first floor. The building was old, but this room had been rebuilt and might have been in a modern office block. It overlooked the High Street, and the sounds of traffic floated in at the open window.

Andrew picked up a pipe and began to fill it.

'Yes, that's the way I feel about it,' he said. 'I suppose I know Paddy almost as well as I know you and Angela. The very thought is preposterous. But the evidence appears to be pretty strong—did you know that?'

'I was in his room when they dug it out.'

'I see.' Andrew sat in silence while he filled his pipe, but before he lit it, he spoke again, giving another faint, tired smile. 'There's something even more preposterous, Jim.'

'Oh, and that is?'

'I've just left Cunningham,' said Andrew. 'He's a good chap, you know. Sound, reliable, sometimes brilliant. He asked me a lot of questions about you. I suppose I am extra-sensitive, but it seemed to me that he was trying to find out whether I thought you were at the receiving end of these burglaries. I hate the thought but you and Angela might be in-

33

volved in all this.'

Jim said: 'It's not entirely a shock.'

'Did you realise they were thinking along those lines?'

'Not at first.' Briefly Jim went over his interview with Lecky, but though Andrew's eyes were steady, he had an uneasy feeling that his friend was not listening. There was something odd in this interview and in Andrew's manner, something which was difficult to define. He wondered why Andrew was so tired; the discovery of the murder had not been made until early morning, it could hardly have upset a night's sleep.

'Well, I rather like the sound of Lecky,' said Andrew, when the story was finished. 'I think you were wise to do what you did.' His pipe had gone out, and he relit it. 'Jim, I'm going to admit what you can already see—this business has knocked me sideways. I had a furious quarrel with the old man last night.'

Jim said slowly: 'Did you?'

'Yes. I haven't yet told the police, but I shall. It was a footling business. You've met his niece Marjorie, haven't you?'

Jim nodded.

'The forty pounds in his wallet were hers,' Andrew went on. 'Repayment of an old debt. Marjorie married against his wishes during the war, and her husband was knocked about pretty badly. They were hard up. Begrudgingly, the old man lent her a hundred and twenty pounds, demanding the repayment of forty pounds every four months. This was the last repayment. He knew as well as I did that she couldn't afford it. Forty pounds or four hundred would have made no difference to him, but——' Andrew paused, and then went on: 'Marjorie will be questioned by the police, I've no doubt, and in any case she'll have to remain in the district for the moment. She and her husband live in London but they are both staying with us at present—I don't think you've met him—he's a very sick man and the snag is that Majorie doesn't get on too well with my mother. I thought of letting them go to an hotel, but somehow I don't think that will quite do and I've been wondering—I know it's a lot to ask—whether you could possibly put them up for the time being.' When Jim did not immediately answer, Andrew went on, still with that faint smile: 'It would show Malling what I thought of the case against

34

O'Hara, you know.'

Jim said slowly: 'How far has the rumour gone that I'm at the receiving end of this business?'

'Well——'

'Pretty far, I imagine,' said Jim. 'Rumour spreads fast in Malling.' He spoke without bitterness, and even seemed faintly amused, but at heart he was troubled. 'You're trying to prove that you don't believe this particular rumour by sending Marjorie and her husband to stay with us. Isn't that it?'

'Yes,' admitted Andrew. 'On the other hand, I do want her to be here. She was also involved in this quarrel. The police are bound to want to ask questions. If she's got to stay in Malling there's nowhere I'd rather she stayed than with you, and the secondary reason gives that added point. Will you have a talk with Angela?' Suddenly his expression altered and his voice became lighter. 'You won't find them a nuisance, I can answer for that. George is a good chap and not by any means helpless. He's liable to sudden heart attacks, but most of the time he's as fit as you or I. Marjorie will gladly lend a hand with the housework.'

'I think perhaps it's a good idea,' Jim said. 'I might have to be out a great deal, and I don't like Angela being in that place alone, with Tub the bundle of mischief he is these days.'

'Splendid! Give me a ring when you've seen Angela—I'll be here until five o'clock.'

'Right!' Jim rose to his feet. 'Nothing else?'

'I may come round for a chat this evening,' said Andrew.

Jim entered the sunlit street, in a thoughtful frame of mind. He knew a little of the story behind Coombs's disapproval of Majorie Grey's marriage. Andrew had etched in the details, that was all.

He guessed that after the previous night's quarrel Andrew had been awake for a long time. He realised what the police might think of that. It was odd that both he and Andrew might be suspected of some part in the murder.

He caught a bus home, arriving a little after four o'clock. Tub came rushing towards him along the drive as Angela hurried out to meet him. He lifted Tug high, perched him on his shoulder, and put his arm round Angela's waist. They strolled back to the house.

35

They were still talking over tea, and Tub, fascinated by a fly on the window, left them in peace. Angela agreed at once to receive Marjorie and her husband, and Jim went to telephone Andrew just before five o'clock. It was while he was waiting for the call to come through that it occurred to him that Cunningham might already know about the quarrel between Andrew and Coombs.

He saw Cunningham as a clever and a dangerous man.

CHAPTER FIVE

NEW ARRIVALS

'What time are they coming?' asked Angela, as Jim replaced the receiver.

'About half-past eight,' said Jim. 'After supper.'

'Well, that was thoughtful, anyhow,' said Angela. 'Darling, are you *very* busy?'

Jim looked wary. 'Why?'

'Well, I thought that if you were going to put work aside for the day you *might* tidy up the sitting-room ...'

Jim laughed, and while Angela was putting Tub to bed, he collected the stray books and papers that lay about, rearranged the flowers with frowning concentration, and straightened the chairs. But he was thinking of Paddy. Paddy liked the house to be full, and made no trouble over extra work. He had declared, in his attractive Irish brogue, that he was as good in the house as any woman and he had proved this over and over again. It was surprising that in so short a time he had established himself so firmly.

Upstairs Tub, too, had suddenly remembered him, and was calling 'Paddy, Paddy!' with increasing determination, until Angela, with a sudden splashing of ducks in his bath water, cleverly diverted him.

'Confound it, I *must* go and see him!' exclaimed Jim.

He was angry with himself for putting off the visit so long. He did not seriously think the police would refuse to allow an interview, but what with Lecky, Andrew and the coming arrival of the Langfords, he had forgotten his intention. He called upstairs to Angela telling her where he was going, then set off.

He hurried along the drive. A bus was due in a few minutes, and if he missed it he would have to walk. Striding down the road he caught sight of a man standing still, half-hidden by shrubbery. He looked at the man again. He was a tall, broad-shouldered fellow, with fair curly hair. Jim had never seen him before. He reached the corner and, with that curly hair in his mind's eye, turned round.

The man was following him.

That gave him a sharp jolt. He hesitated by the bus-stop, not quite certain whether to walk after all; if he walked he would know for certain whether the other was actually watching him.

The bus was coming along. Jim decided to catch it. The lower deck was full and he had to go upstairs; and the curly-haired man followed him.

As the bus moved off, Jim could see along the avenue; another man was standing opposite his house.

Did that mean that two policemen were watching him and Angela?

The curly-haired man sat two seats behind him. There seemed no way of proving whether he was a policeman or not. Jim pondered over it during the journey and then, at the outskirts of Malling, leapt to his feet, giving the other no warning. Nevertheless, when he arrived on the pavement, the fair-haired man was behind him.

There was still no proof that he was a policeman, but as Jim neared the police station he thought of a way in which he might find out. He turned into the building, and then waited in the hall. A uniformed policeman on duty saluted the curly-haired man.

'So that's that,' muttered Jim. He asked for Cunningham, and was taken upstairs immediately.

It was the first time he had seen the detective-sergeant out of uniform. He waved to a chair.

'Sit down, Mr. Gantry.'

'Thanks,' said Jim. 'I really want to see the Inspector.'

'He's off duty,' said Cunningham, 'and I'm in temporary charge of the case, Mr. Gantry. How can I help you?'

Jim said: 'I would like to see O'Hara.'

'Well, that's all right,' said Cunningham, pleasantly. 'You understand, I take it, that you won't be able to see him alone?'

'Of course,' said Jim, relieved by the promptness with

which his request had been granted, but still annoyed that Cunningham had not told him earlier that Paddy was wanted for murder. 'You misled me this morning, didn't you?'

'*Misled* you?' repeated Cunningham innocently.

'By withholding your real reason for searching Paddy's room.'

Cunningham's eyebrows rose a little.

'Information withheld by the police is not quite the same as information withheld *to* them,' he said pleasantly. 'However, I'm rather glad you've looked in. I wanted a word with you about O'Hara's defence. Tomorrow, as I expect you know, he will only come up for a first hearing at the magistrate's court and there will probably be a remand until after the inquest, but you may want someone there to watch his interests.'

'I'm taking Andrew Dale's advice about that,' answered Jim.

'Oh,' said Cunningham. He stood up. 'You couldn't get better advice.' He did not refer to his earlier suggestion that Jim should avoid Andrew. 'Well, let's go along and see O'Hara.'

He was very informal, but Jim was grimly conscious of the possibility that he was deliberately trying to disarm him. They walked silently through the long passages of the police station, until they came to a door outside which a policeman was standing.

'All right, Symes,' said Cunningham.

Symes opened the door. It led to a wider passage with several cells on either side. Only one appeared to be occupied. Near it was a small desk and a chair, at which a uniformed policeman was sitting. He got up promptly.

Paddy O'Hara was lying on a narrow bed, smoking, his hands clasped behind his head, his eyes closed.

Not until the policeman put the key in the lock did Paddy open his eyes. Then, in a flash, he was off the bed and at the door, his round ugly face split by a smile.

'Why, sir, it's a great pleasure to see you, that it is,' declared Paddy, delightedly. 'And how's Mrs. Gantry and the young imp? He hasn't been falling down and hurting himself again today, has he now?'

'No, he's fine,' said Jim.

'And that's what I want to hear,' declared Paddy. 'I've been lying here half-asleep, Mr. Gantry, thinking about the boy,

39

that I have. And him so gay and happy and me locked in a cell with only that moon-faced policeman to look at and they not giving me more than a word now and again. I ask ye, Mr. Gantry, would you like it?'

Jim shook his head, smiling.

'And nor do I,' declared Paddy. 'When I'm out of this place I'll be telling them what I think of them, Mr. Gantry, and no mistake.' He grinned impishly at Cunningham. 'I wouldn't mind so much but for one thing,' he went on. 'They call me a liar, and I don't like the man who calls me a liar, I never did and I never will.'

'Who's called you a liar?' demanded Cunningham.

'Why, and sure you did yourself,' accused Paddy. 'I told you I've never done a single thing in all my life to deserve being put in prison, and here I am in prison, so it's a liar you're calling me! Am I to go out now?' he demanded, eagerly.

'I'm afraid you'll have to stay,' said Cunningham.

'Well, I expected no more, so it's not a disappointment,' Paddy said with a shrug. 'Mr. Gantry, there's one thing you can be doing for me, send me in a packet of cigarettes, I'm down to me last two and I wouldn't ask the policeman because before I know where I am they'll be accusing me of trying to obtain goods by false pretences, that they will, me having no money, and I as honest as the day is long as doubtless you've told them.'

'I've told them,' said Jim, 'and I'll get the cigarettes.'

'And I'll be thanking you,' said Paddy, warmly. 'Well, it's a fine mess I've got myself into and no mistake. By the Holy Mother, what a mess it is, and me as innocent as a child.'

'I think you'll find the police very fair,' Jim said.

'Fair?' Paddy raised his eyes to the ceiling. ''Tis a word they wouldn't be understanding.'

Jim wished he would stop teasing Cunningham and the policeman on duty. The glint in Paddy's eyes told him that it was no more than teasing, but it might affect their treatment of him, denying him those little favours and privileges which would otherwise come his way. But when he glanced at Cunningham, Jim saw an amused smile, and his fears were quietened.

'Now there's one thing I've been wanting to see you about,' declared Paddy. 'It's this, Mr. Gantry, and I mean every word of it. You're not to go spending a lot of money to get me out of here. You've no money to throw about, as I well know, and it wouldn't be easy on me conscience if ye were to do that—ye'll promise me, Mr. Gantry?'

'Not a penny more than is necessary,' said Jim.

'Now that's fine,' said Paddy. 'Fine! I'll not be needing a lawyer, they're scoundrels to a man, excepting Mr. Dale he being a friend of yours, sir, and I can talk to the judge as well as any lawyer in the country and better than most, but if you want to say a word yourself then I'll not say no.'

'Mr. Dale will probably see you before you go into court,' Jim said, 'and you must do what he tells you, Paddy.'

'Mr. Dale himself? There's a fine gentleman for you!' He stabbed a finger at Cunningham. 'That's what I call a real fine gentleman, his own friend lying dead and me accused of the wicked deed and he will help me. You'll thank him for me, Mr. Gantry?'

'Yes,' Jim promised.

For the first time he saw beneath the façade of high spirits the anxiety which lurked in Paddy's mind. The smile was still there and the voice was the same, but fear showed itself, in his almost pathetic gratitude.

There was so little to be said, and Jim wondered awkwardly how to break off the interview. In the pause, Cunningham said:

'I'm afraid the time is up, Mr. Gantry.'

'There he is, at it again,' said Paddy, 'and here am I sitting on my backside doing nothing and Mrs. Gantry worked to death at the house and Tub not tucked up like he usually is, and ye have to go, before we've said a quarter of what's in our minds. But it was good of ye to come and see me, Mr. Gantry, though no more than I expected.'

Jim said: 'Paddy, listen to me. You are not to worry.'

'Now should I worry with two fine gentlemen like you and Mr. Dale by my side?' demanded Paddy. 'God watch over you.'

Jim and Cunningham were in the front hall before Jim could trust himself to speak. He was conscious of Cunningham's interested gaze and angry with himself for being so affected. Yet affected he was; he would have felt ten times better had Paddy ranted and raged.

He sought for something sensible to say.

'Will he be able to smoke after the remand, Cunningham?'

'If we keep him here, and we probably shall,' said Cunningham. 'I'll look after those cigarettes.'

'Thanks.' Jim took out a pound note. 'That will keep him going. What time will the hearing be in the morning?'

'Eleven o'clock.'

'Thanks.'

Jim said: 'Look here, Cunningham, I've never believed that Paddy committed those burglaries and I'm quite sure he didn't kill Coombs. You'll look at both sides of the evidence, won't you?'

'You needn't worry about that,' Cunningham said. 'And Andrew Dale won't make any mistakes, you know.'

'Thanks,' said Jim.

It was a little after seven o'clock when he caught the bus, but it was not until he was walking along the avenue that he noticed the curly-haired man followed him, and when he reached his house he saw the other man standing in the shrubbery opposite, watching.

Angela came hurrying along the drive, eager and anxious.

'How is he, Jim?'

'He made me want to cry,' said Jim.

'Oh.' Angela tucked her arm into his. 'Poor Paddy. Jim, you don't think he's in real danger, do you?'

Jim said: 'I think he's in grave danger.'

They were silent over the meal. Jim wished that he had not been so gloomy, but experience told him that in the long run it was better to tell Angela just how he felt.

At eight o'clock they washed up together, and Jim was already feeling the depression lifting.

Angela, making coffee, looked round at him as he wiped a plate.

'We'll see him through, darling.'

'Of course we will!'

Her eyes sparkled. 'That's better! Now, exactly what did he say? We've got twenty minutes before the Langfords come.

Oh! I've forgotten to put the hot-water bottle in! Put a kettle on, darling.'

She was still upstairs when he heard their arrival. Jim opened the front door while Andrew and the Langfords were getting out of the car. When Marjorie turned, as Andrew said: 'Here we are, Jim!' she did so quickly and gracefully. She had an elfin, piquant face with great violet eyes, dark wavy hair and a lovely complexion. She smiled, a little diffidently.

'Hallo, Mrs. Langford,' said Jim, warmly.

They shook hands, then Andrew introduced George Langford. A thin, white hand rested in Jim's for a moment. The man looked sad as well as ill; the contrast between him and the vitality of his lively wife was astonishing and a little hurtful.

Langford had a deep voice, and spoke slowly.

'This is very good of you, Gantry.'

'We're very glad to have you,' said Jim.

At this moment Angela came running down the stairs.

'Hallo, everybody! Marjorie, my dear, how nice to see you!' As she had seldom met Marjorie, that was a promising start. 'And Mr. Langford——'

A faint smile played at Langford's lips.

'May I be called George?'

'Thank heavens, you may indeed,' exclaimed Angela. 'I could not have kept up the Mr. Langford for long!'

They were soon in the sitting-room, where coffee was waiting, chatting pleasantly. George Langford had the least to say. He sat back in an easy-chair as if he really needed the rest. Jim sensed a tragedy deeper and greater then he had realised. It was reflected in Marjorie's smile whenever she looked at her husband; and sometimes Jim saw her glance towards Andrew with an odd expression.

'And now I'm going to take Marjorie up to her room,' Angela said. 'We won't be long.'

The three men sat in silence for a few minutes, Andrew and Jim smoking. Then George said:

'Seriously, I do appreciate this.'

'We do, too,' Jim said. 'I especially so. I was rather worried about Angela being left on her own.'

Andrew looked at his watch.

'I ought to be getting back,' he said.

'I suppose you must. But before you go, what about Paddy tomorrow? Will he want a formal defence?'

'No. He only needs to plead not guilty, and say nothing else—if he'll have the sense to do that.' He smiled. 'I was going to suggest that I looked in to see him this evening. A word of warning not to talk too much might not come amiss.' He leapt from his seat. 'Well, I must be going. Don't get up any of you—you're all tired. I'll let myself out.'

As Angela and Marjorie came down the stairs, he slipped away and Jim dropped back into his chair from which he had half-risen.

'Do either of you play?' asked Angela, looking at the upright piano. 'Jim can, but seldom does.'

'George plays,' Marjorie said. 'I vamp a bit.'

'This is promising,' said Jim.

George *could* play. He needed no music, but sat at the piano and held them fascinated with his mastery; even Majorie was absorbed. All three watched those white hands moving over the keys. Jim, sitting back, felt depression seep from him. He saw Angela smiling with delight, and Marjorie, curled up on the settee, half-closing her eyes in peaceful contentment. When George stopped, the silence was intense. It seemed to last for a long time, and it was broken by the sound of a door shutting upstairs.

CHAPTER SIX

INTRUDER

'What's that?' cried Angela, jumping to her feet.

'Only a door,' said Jim.

'Someone must have closed it.'

'The wind——'

'There *isn't* any wind.'

Silence fell again, and then was broken by the sound of footsteps above their heads.

'There is someone there!' cried Angela. 'Darling!' Jim had started to move. 'Darling, take something with you, take a poker, take——'

Jim was already in the hall. The light was on, and he could see the landing. No one was there. He could hear movements in the room above. He thought of the curly-haired policeman; had he allowed someone to break in?

He found George by his side.

'Leave this to me, old chap,' he said. 'Look after the girls.'

He started up the stairs, his heart hammering, and by the time he got to the top he wished he had taken Angela's advice. There was no light on the landing. The switch was at the foot of the second flight of stairs, some distance away from him. He crept slowly towards it, then pressed it down.

Nothing happened!

'Put on the light!' cried Angela. 'I'm going up to Tub, anything might happen to him!'

'Stay down there,' ordered Jim. 'Open the front door and call "Police"—just as loud as you can.'

As he heard Angela run across the hall, he listened for nearer sounds. There were none, until the moment Angela called out; and then he heard a window open. It came from the Langfords' room. He hurried towards it. The door was closed.

45

He opened it cautiously. There was no light in the room, but enough filtered in from the street lamps to show the figure of a man, his back towards him, climbing out of the window.

As Jim rushed forward, the man made a frantic attempt to clear the window; but he was in an awkward position. Jim reached him and grabbed his wrist.

Angela was still yelling 'Police! Police!' and someone was running across the road. The man in the window did not move; it was as if he realised that the game was up. The footsteps left the pavement and sounded on the drive. Jim opened his lips to tell them where he was, when the man back-heeled and caught him in the stomach. The pain was so sudden and acute that Jim relaxed his grip. The man wrenched himself free and kicked again. Jim fell backwards into the room. He heard confused voices downstairs, and then footsteps coming up.

'Front garden!' he called out, hoarsely. 'Front garden!'

But his words did not reach the man who came hurrying into the room—the curly-haired man who had been on duty during the afternoon.

'Where——' he began.

'Window!' gasped Jim.

The curly-haired man rushed to the window and called out: 'Look out, down there!' Did that mean there was another policeman on duty outside, and that there was still a chance of catching the intruder? Jim got up unsteadily. He heard the sounds of men running, of heavy breathing. Then Angela and Marjorie burst into the room.

'Jim!'

'I'm all right,' murmured Jim.

'What on earth is he *doing*?' demanded Angela, looking at the window.

The curly-haired man was climbing out. He disappeared and dropped down; they heard him land on the drive.

'Let's hope he has more luck than I had,' said Jim, ruefully. With a hand on his stomach he walked towards the door. Angela had gone to the nursery to Tub, who was sleeping soundly through it all. 'I suppose he thought this was the best room to get out of,' he murmured. He put the bulb back and switched on the light, then stopped, seeing the two open suit-cases, their contents strewn about the floor.

He realised for the first time that the intruder had come to search the Langfords' luggage.

Jim himself was bemused, Angela and Marjorie seemed struck dumb by the burglary, and in that emergency, while they waited downstairs for news from the fair-haired police-man, George proved his usefulness. Calm, even mildly amused, he had a soothing effect on Angela.

'If that was a policeman,' he said, 'it's out of our hands and we needn't worry about reporting it. You're sure he was a policeman, Jim?'

'Yes.'

'Well, I've seen him in the street several times today,' said Angela. 'I thought he was rather suspicious-looking. I wanted to tell you, darling, but I forgot in the rush. Has he been watching us?'

'Probably,' said George.

'Oh,' said Angela, in a small voice. 'We are having a time, aren't we?'

George said: 'Well, obviously they're going to watch the house where Paddy lived. They would think that some accom-plice might not know that he's under arrest and come to see him.

'I suppose so,' admitted Angela.

'I wonder if the—the man who broke in had anything to do with the other burglaries?' remarked Marjorie.

'Well, anyhow, it proves that there's another burglar about besides Paddy, and that's something in his favour,' said George. Unruffled, smiling, he went on: 'It's peculiar to think that our cases were rifled, isn't it?'

'More than peculiar, it's unpleasant,' said Marjorie.

'I don't suppose he knew they were your cases,' said Jim.

'They're marked plainly enough,' George told him. 'And you said that nothing else had been touched.'

'As far as I could tell,' Jim admitted. 'When the police come, we'll look round more thoroughly.' He got up. 'Some-one's coming, I think.' He went out to the hall. The front door was open and he could see the fair-haired man walking along the drive. There was a chastened look about the fellow, and Jim did not need telling that the burglar had escaped.

'Hallo,' he greeted. 'No luck?'

'I'm afraid not,' said the other. 'I was just too late. Is everyone all right, Mr. Gantry?'

'Yes. I've a bruise or two, that's all.'

'I could kick myself,' confessed the policeman. 'I can't imagine how he got up to the house without being seen. We've been watching it front and back.'

'Whom do you mean by "we"?'

The other smiled. 'Sorry, but I thought you knew. I'm Detective-Sergeant Owen, Malshire C.I.D.' He went on: 'I've been brought in from Linton to lend a hand. Did you get a good view of the man?'

'No, a very poor one, I'm afraid. He'd taken the globes out of their sockets, so there was no light.'

'He was a fly customer all right,' said Owen. 'I've sent my man after him, but I don't think it will do much good. Do you mind if I use your telephone?'

'It's behind you,' said Jim.

Half an hour afterwards, Cunningham arrived. Not until then was a thorough search made. While it was being carried out, Marjorie, George and Angela stayed downstairs. The others went from room to room, until Jim was satisfied that the intruder had been interested only in the Langfords' luggage.

'I ought to have come straight up to this room,' he confessed. 'The door doesn't stay open unless it's held by something, and it swings to with a bang. The footsteps were immediately over our heads in the sitting-room, too.'

Cunningham said: 'Did you hear the footsteps immediately after the door shut?'

'Yes.'

Cunningham smiled. 'It probably startled him and he rushed to the window. Then he kept quiet, hoping you hadn't heard him.' He looked down at the open cases. There was a pair of silver-backed hair-brushes, some books, slippers and shoes. One case had been half-emptied, but the other was still neatly packed, a dress in tissue paper on top. 'Well, you didn't give him time to do much,' said Cunningham, 'I suppose that's

48

an advantage. Do Mr. or Mrs. Langford know what he wanted?'

'I don't think so,' said Jim. 'I suppose you'll want a word with them.'

'Yes.'

'You'll bear in mind that Langford's a sick man, won't you?' asked Jim.

Cunningham nodded, unsurprised, an indication that he knew something about the Langfords; there was no telling how far his inquiries had gone. 'Are they staying here for long, Mr. Gantry?'

'Indefinitely,' said Jim, 'and at Mr. Dale's suggestion.'

'I see, sir.'

Cunningham did not ask George or Marjorie any questions, but requested them to look through their cases to make sure that nothing was missing. As he stood watching, Jim thought that he was showing great interest in everything there; it was as if he were looking for something which he expected George would try to conceal. The whole search lasted for nearly half an hour, and then George straightened up.

'Nothing's missing,' he said briefly.

'Have you any idea what they came for?'

'No idea at all.'

'I see, sir, thank you.' Cunningham turned to Jim. 'I'm extremely sorry that this was allowed to happen,' he said. 'It's a very dark night, and the man probably came over from the next-door garden.'

'Probably,' said Jim. 'Not very good police work, all the same.'

'Accidents will happen,' said Cunningham.

'Accidents, yes,' said Jim. 'This time it was a mistaken policy, I think. You were watching only for those of us who left the house, weren't you?' Jim spoke so sharply that Angela looked up in astonishment. 'Why the devil must you beat about the bush? You think that I helped O'Hara and was connected with these burglaries and you expected me to try and get in touch with someone else. Isn't that the truth?'

Cunningham said: 'It was considered necessary to watch the house in everyone's interest, Mr. Gantry.'

'Oh, all right,' said Jim, already repenting his sudden out-

49

burst. 'I suppose you know your job. But if you think us worth watching, you might do it properly.'

Cunningham said no more. He went out, Jim closing the door firmly behind him.

Angela came out of the sitting-room, and said: 'I've decided I don't like that man in spite of his good looks. Come upstairs to see Tub with me, will you? I don't like going up there on my own.'

'Of course,' said Jim. 'We won't be long,' he called out to the others, and then he led the way upstairs. Tub was sleeping with one arm and one leg outside the bedclothes.

'Bless him!' exclaimed Angela, and Tub sighed heavily as she tucked him in. In the passage, she said: 'Darling, why do you think that burglar came?'

'It's not much use guessing,' said Jim, 'and that's all it would be. I'm more interested in finding out why the police think he came. I wish I hadn't flared up.'

'Well, you were quite right,' Angela assured him with wifely partiality. 'They ought to do the job properly if they're going to do it at all. I shan't have much faith in the police after this.' They walked to the head of the stairs. 'Darling——'

'Hm-hm?'

'What do you think of George and Marjorie?'

'Well he's obviously a sick man.'

'Yes, I know. Do you like him?'

'I think I might come to like him. He certainly doesn't wear his heart on his sleeve.'

'No, he *certainly* doesn't,' said Angela, significantly.

'What on earth do you mean?'

'Do you mean to tell me you can't *see* what's the matter?' demanded Angela. 'Couldn't you sense the tension when they first arrived?'

'I did notice something, but——'

'You wouldn't notice anything if it weren't right under your nose,' declared Angela, with an air of satisfied resignation.

'Here and now you will tell me what you're talking about,' said Jim, firmly.

'But it was so obvious,' said Angela. 'The way they looked at one another, the tension, the——'

'*What do you mean?*'

50

Angela said: 'But, darling, Andrew and Marjorie are in love with each other. George knows it. It must be heartbreaking, mustn't it, because anyone could see—even you,' she added, with a catch in her voice, 'that George is in love with Marjorie, too.'

CHHAPTER SEVEN

GEORGE

Jim wished that Angela had not chosen that moment to tell him. They had to go downstairs and talk naturally to the Langfords, and that would not be easy when he was so conscious of the cause of the earlier restraint. He did not doubt Angela's diagnosis. As she had spoken, he had realised how right she was. Yet he was puzzled that these people allowed it to be so obvious to anyone with a discerning eye. Perhaps the murder of old Coombs had inflamed the situation, creating an emotional tension in which it had been difficult to hide the truth.

'Darling, don't let them see we know about this, will you?' asked Angela.

Jim laughed. 'Don't be a goop. Of course I won't.'

'Well, mind you don't,' said Angela. 'I wonder if they'd like a cup of tea? I'll go and put the kettle on,' she decided, and pushed him towards the sitting-room door. 'You keep them company, we can't leave them on their own too long.'

'Coward!' hissed Jim. He knew she was as embarrassed as he, and smiled ruefully.

Summoning all his resources he went in. George was sitting in an easy-chair and Marjorie was standing over him. She looked round.

'It's nothing,' she said, 'he'll be all right in a few minutes, it's nothing.' But there was agony in her voice.

In sudden alarm, Jim stepped forward to look at George. He had a shock. George's eyes were wide open, but he sat absolutely rigid. His face was like yellow parchment, with a blue tinge at lips and nostrils. He was breathing with difficulty.

'Can I do anything?' Jim asked, tensely.

52

'No. That is, if he could have a cup of something hot in a few minutes it will help him.'

'Angela's making some tea.'

'Oh, that's splendid.' Marjorie turned and looked at him, and there were tears in her eyes. 'I'm so sorry it happened tonight, Jim. He hasn't had a turn for several weeks.'

'I expect it was the excitement,' said Jim, lamely.

'That is probably what it was, but perhaps it would be better if Angela didn't see him like this. I'll go out and get the tea, and explain things to her.'

'If you prefer it,' said Jim.

'I think I would.' Marjorie looked down at her husband. 'Darling, you won't mind being left alone with Jim for a few moments, will you?'

George's almost colourless lips moved. 'No.'

'I'll get you some tea.' Marjorie's voice was unsteady. She turned and hurried away.

Jim pulled up a chair and sat down, feeling helpless, and at a loss. The big room, with its old-fashioned furniture, was very quiet. Following the burglary, this attack seemed the last straw. Marjorie's manner was so odd, too. Why had she hurried away? It was almost as if she had fled from the sight of George's face. The whole situation was beyond him.

He smiled at the sick man.

'Good—of—you,' George said. His voice was barely audible. He beckoned Jim, who helped him to sit up. 'Thanks. It's nearly over now.'

George was sweating freely, but his colour was better; his voice was firmer, too. He moved his legs cautiously, and began to move his hand.

'Cigarette?' asked Jim.

'Not allowed,' said George. 'I'm very sorry—about this.'

'Now—please——'

'But I am. Must upset you. Marjorie's used to it.' He looked towards the door. There was a pause, an odd kind of pause; it was as if George were gathering his strength for some great effort. 'If I had any guts, I'd finish myself off.'

'Now look here——'

'It would be the sensible thing to do.' The voice was much stronger and George even waved his hand to emphasise his words. 'I'm useless. I shall always be useless. I might live for ten or twenty years and never be anything but an invalid. Oh, they *say* I'll get better. Marjorie *says* I will. She's ruined herself trying to make me better. And now she's under suspicion of murder because I——'

Jim said: 'Steady, George.'

There was another tense pause, before George spoke again.

'That's all quite true you know, Gantry.'

'Marjorie can hardly be under suspicion of murder if the police are so sure that Paddy O'Hara committed it.'

'They may think she put him up to it,' George said.

'But that's absurd!'

'Not really.' The dispassionate voice was compelling. 'I've been like this for three years. Marjorie has spent a fortune on specialists. She even borrowed from Coombs—I wish to heaven I'd known that before, I wouldn't have allowed it. The old devil was——' He broke off, with a grim smile. 'If I talk like this, I shall lay myself open to a charge of murder, shan't I? I don't mind admitting that when I heard he was dead, I rejoiced.'

Jim said nothing.

'And then I realised what might follow,' George went on. 'Have you heard about the quarrel last night? Andrew tried to persuade Coombs to make the money a gift, Coombs refused, there was a furious row. Marjorie was there. A servant heard it, that's why the police are watching Marjorie *and* Andrew, although I think they're so impressed by Andrew's position in the town that they haven't the courage to do anything openly about him.'

Jim said: 'That wouldn't worry them.'

'I wonder,' said George. His lips twisted. 'I feel better now I've got that off my chest. Once again—I'm sorry that I burdened you with it.'

'That's all right.'

'And I don't think I'm likely to have another attack for a month or more,' George continued. 'You needn't have any fear about that. Only one thing I do ask.'

'What's that?'

'If we become a nuisance, throw us out.'

'My dear fellow,' said Jim, 'you're talking out of the back of your neck. You're not going to be a nuisance. Marjorie and Angela have hit it off already, and when I want to work I shall go upstairs and leave you to your own devices. As a matter of fact, I'm very glad you're here for one reason I haven't yet told you.'

'What is it?' asked George.

Jim said: 'If there is any kind of suspicion against you and Marjorie and, presumably, Andrew, police attention will be focused on this house. I'm very keen to know what goes on. I suppose you know that they think I employ Paddy to go out burgling?'

George smiled. 'Andrew said that they thought it possible.'

'I'm glad he warned you about that,' went on Jim. 'Now, let's forget it. Are you really feeling better?'

'I shall be more lively tomorrow than I have been for weeks,' George told him. 'An attack seems to get something out of my system. Provided I don't overdo it, I shall be almost as fit as you in the next few days.' He was certainly looking very much better. As he sat up, the door opened to admit Angela and Marjorie, with the tea.

Jim watched Angela pouring out rather thoughtfully. Marjorie must have known how quick the recovery would be; why, then, had she made such a fuss? He came to the conclusion that she had wanted them to be on their own for a while.

Then he found himself wondering why the Langfords' room had been burgled, and what the burglar had expected to find in their luggage.

It was half-past nine before Cunningham and his friend, the curly-haired watcher, reached the police station. Owen had been relieved by a man for the night, but he was still smarting under his failure to have seen, and caught, the burglar. Cunningham sympathised with his feelings. Until the call from Owen at the Gantrys' house the day had gone perfectly. Still elated by being left in charge of the case, Cunningham had applied for and obtained Reg Owen's services. The two men, being such close friends, had looked forward to a joint triumph. Now Owen had slipped up badly and not only injured his own reputation but had probably earned Cunningham a reprimand.

'Maitland won't be pleased because I've kept him waiting,' Cunningham said. 'He told me to ring him at nine o'clock.'

'He can't expect you to work like a clock,' said Owen.

'That's the trouble: he does.' They reached the office and Cunningham put in the call. He had to hold on for some time, then Maitland's stern voice answered him.

'I'm sorry I'm late, sir,' said Cunningham, 'but we had some more excitement.'

'And that was?' Maitland asked him.

'A burglary at the Gantrys' house,' Cunningham said. 'We missed our man, I'm afraid, sir, although we were watching the house. It was a bad slip.'

There was a pause. Cunningham grimaced rather unhappily at Owen.

'Was this burglary on the same lines as the earlier ones?' asked Maitland, no trace of annoyance showing in his voice.

'Very similar, sir, except that a ladder wasn't used. The house is easy to break into, and a window on the first floor was open.'

Maitland said: 'You'd better come over and see me, Cunningham.'

That meant nearly an hour's drive across country. Cunningham was on the road five minutes later, leaving Owen to make a full report of the burglary. As he drove, he turned the whole affair over in his mind.

The road was a good one and there was little traffic. He reached Langham three-quarters of an hour later; luckily, Maitland's home was on the southern outskirts, an attractive house with creeper-clad walls and latticed windows.

The door opened before Cunningham rang the bell. A short, dark manservant said: 'Sergeant Cunningham?'

'Yes.'

'The Colonel is waiting.' 'Old soldier' guessed Cunningham, for the man carried himself as if on parade.

He was led up the stairs to a large, book-lined room warmed by a small log fire. Maitland was sitting in an easy chair, with whisky and soda by his side. He indicated a chair opposite him.

'Sit down, Cunningham.' He poured drinks and handed one to Cunningham, who had not expected this homely hospitality.

'Now, what made you slip up with that burglar?' he asked.

'I think the truth is, sir, that the men were watching specifically for anyone who came out of the house, or called in the normal way; they weren't expecting a cat burglar.'

'I see. We can't afford too many mistakes, you know. What was the thief after?'

'That's the curious part of it,' said Cunningham. 'He went straight to the room where the Gantrys had put the Langfords...'

Cunningham told the story tersely and well; not until he finished did he pause, very conscious, then, of the Colonel's steady gaze.

'I see,' said Maitland. 'You feel sure that the thief went there only to get something from the Langfords?'

'I do, sir.'

'Who, if O'Hara is innocent, had a motive for killing Coombs and might possibly have killed him,' mused Maitland. 'And there is the curious fact that Andrew Dale arranged for these two families to be together. You say that Dale's mother disliked Mrs. Langford?'

'Yes, sir.'

'How did you find that out?'

Cunningham smiled. 'The usual back-door method, sir!'

'I see. The servants talked. We are finding ourselves in rather deeper waters than we expected, aren't we? To sum up: there are two groups of suspects, with a possible third. The Gantry–O'Hara group, which would provide a robbery motive; the Langford group, with an emotional motive, since Coombs was apparently bitter and vindictive against his niece because of her marriage to an invalid; and, as the outsider, Andrew Dale, who is known to have quarrelled with his partner after taking Mrs. Langford's side in the earlier row.'

'That is the position, sir,' agreed Cunningham. 'Of course, the repayment of part of a loan is hardly a motive for murder, but according to the reports I've had, the quarrel between Mrs. Langford and Mr. Coombs was extremely violent and bitter. So was the later quarrel between Mr. Dale and Mr. Coombs. I don't know whether Mr. Langford—the innocent cause of the whole thing—has been fully informed of what happened or not.'

'What about Coombs's will?'

'None has been found yet, sir.'

'We can't close our list of suspects until it has been,' said Maitland. 'I wonder——'

Cunningham explained: 'Could *that* be it?' in such a startled tone that, involuntarily, Maitland smiled.

'Could what be what?'

'Sorry, sir. It suddenly struck me that the thief might have been looking for the will,' said Cunningham, eagerly. 'It could easily be hidden in a suitcase. One of the cases might have a false bottom, or a partition which I didn't see tonight. The will might have been stolen—it *is* odd that we haven't found it yet, although we've been through Mr. Coombs's private papers thoroughly.'

'You may be right,' said Maitland, and added drily: 'It's a pity you didn't think of it while you were at the Gantrys', you would have had an excuse for a thorough search there, too. Well, it can't be helped. And we have to make sure that the will is missing before we can say that someone tried to steal it. You've asked Dale about it, I suppose?'

'Oh yes. And tomorrow we'll search Coombs's office.'

'What is your impression of Dale?' Maitland asked.

Cunningham considered carefully before he spoke.

'Well, sir, I have the greatest respect and liking for him. I know him fairly well. He is shrewd—in fact I think he is brilliant, sir, he would probably do well in a larger town, but for some reason or another he has always refused to leave Malling. Normally I wouldn't hesitate to say that it would be absurd to suspect him, but he *has* behaved rather oddly. It isn't surprising that the murder affected him, and yet—why did he send the Langfords to stay with the Gantrys? Was it wholly because his mother and Mrs. Langford didn't get on well, or was there another reason? Then, he's prepared to look after O'Hara's interests. Well, *would* he, if he knew there was a reasonable likelihood that O'Hara had killed his partner? I don't think so, sir. Lawyers are pretty cold-blooded, but that would be going a bit too far. He might want to help O'Hara, though, if he knows that O'Hara is innocent.'

'Yes,' said Maitland.

'But if O'Hara *is* innocent, then someone is framing him,'

Cunningham pointed out. 'It surely can't be Dale; he would hardly frame a man one moment and undertake his defence the next. And while I can believe that the Langfords might have killed Coombs if they were worked up to a pitch of desperation, they certainly wouldn't set out to frame O'Hara. It wouldn't be in character. That all suggests that there is someone we haven't yet thought of, sir.'

'I suppose you're right,' admitted Maitland. 'It's a pity. We've quite enough complications as it is.'

'We might as well face the worst,' said Cunningham, grimly.

'Yes, well about this betting which O'Hara claims to have done. Have you interviewed his bookmaker yet?'

'No, sir,' said Cunningham. 'Porton, the bookmaker concerned, is at Newmarket. He's closed his office for a day or two. I'm told that he's due back tomorrow.'

'Rather a convenient time to close his office, wasn't it?'

'He has done it before,' said Cunningham. 'He employs part-time workers and one regular clerk, who's gone with him. I can't get any information from the part-timers, and in any case they might not know whether Paddy O'Hara has an account with the firm or not. Porton's worked in Malling for twenty years, sir, and he has a good reputation.'

'I see. Tell me, Cunningham, if O'Hara isn't the thief, have you anyone else in mind?'

'No one at all, sir.'

'It seems to me that you've a long way to go yet,' said Maitland. 'I've spoken to Mrs. Forrest,' he added, apparently irrelevantly, 'and Inspector Forrest has influenza; he'll be off duty for a fortnight at least. Don't you think we ought to ask Scotland Yard for help?'

The question came as a complete surprise, and startled Cunningham, whose disappointment was the greater because he had seemed to be getting on so well with Maitland. Now he looked into the other's handsome face and steady, expressionless grey eyes, and turned the question over in his mind. In the excitement of telling his story and eagerness to make sure that he missed nothing, he had not realised that he was weakening his own case. Now, he saw only too clearly what Maitland feared. He would soon be wallowing in a welter of denials, false trails and irrelevancies, and might be unable to cope.

Maitland was right; first-class help was needed.

'I suppose we should, sir,' he said at last.

Maitland smiled. 'I'm glad you said that, Cunningham. The job is the thing, not personal hopes and ambitions. But there will be an advantage for you, you know. You will be in charge of the local force working on the case, and where things go wrong you will have an older and more experienced man to help you. But I want to pick my man, if I can——' The little twinkle showed in his eyes and disappeared. 'I will go to London tomorrow, see the Assistant Commissioner, and try to make sure you get someone with whom it will be easy to work.'

'You're very good, sir.'

'I don't want Scotland Yard to have all the credit for any success we may have, you know,' said Maitland. He looked at his watch. 'You'd better be off, you won't be home until midnight. Don't overdo it. You'll be matching your wits against Scotland Yard as well as the murderer, so you want to keep fresh.' He got up. 'Goodnight, Cunningham, and good luck.'

'Thank you, sir,' said Cunningham.

As he drove homewards, he was smiling. If Forrest had delivered that blow, he would have felt furiously angry, but Maitland had managed to soften it and even to make the prospect seem attractive. The Colonel was certainly not living up to his reputation.

Cunningham was several miles from Malling when he saw the glow in the sky. It puzzled him at first, and then alarmed him; somewhere in the centre of the town there was a fire of some proportions. A mile further on he could see leaping flames and great clouds of smoke. He drove quickly, hearing the clang of fire-bells as he drew nearer.

Then he turned into the High Street, and saw that the offices of *Dale, Coombs and Dale* were blazing furiously.

CHAPTER EIGHT

ARSON

Cunningham got out of his car a hundred yards from the building. A fresh burst of fire sent a wave of hot air into his face, and made him gasp. A crowd at least a hundred strong was pressing about the firemen, and he saw a few policemen trying to force them further away. An escape was run up to the top of the building; obviously the fire had started at the bottom; although the front was nearly gutted the top floor was, outwardly at least, hardly touched.

A fireman passed him.

'Is someone up there?' he demanded.

'Why don't you go home?' growled the fireman. 'Haven't you got something better to do than gape?' He pushed his way forward, while Cunningham hurried nearer to the spot, encountering P.C. Small, who failed to recognise him at first and snapped:

'I told you to stand back!'

'All right, Small,' said Cunningham.

'Sorry, Sergeant, I——'

'That's all right. Get the crowd away if you can.'

He went ahead, keeping one hand in front of his face to shield it from the heat. Hoses were being sprayed on to the buildings on either side, but one of them was already alight. There was a small fire on the roof of the Malling Restaurant, and two firemen were climbing a ladder to get to it. In the lurid glare, the frightened, fascinated faces of the crowd seemed grotesque. He saw the proprietress of the restaurant opening the door, then turned his attention to the offices of *Dale, Coombs and Dale*, and the fire-escape which rose high above his head.

He recognised Williams, the local N.F.S. Captain.

'Who's up there?' he asked.

'Andrew Dale.'

Cunningham drew in his breath. 'What are the chances?'

'Ten to one *against*,' growled Williams.

Cunningham stood back and watched. The flames were getting higher, and almost hid the top of the building from sight. He could not see any of the windows, and there was no sign of Andrew Dale. Apparently the people on the other side of the escape had a clearer view, for suddenly there came a roar of mingled alarm and excitement, followed by a rush from the spot as burning timbers broke away from the building. One such timber struck the fire-escape. For a moment it was hidden by smoke.

Williams said: 'Well, that's that.'

'Are you sure——'

'Of course I'm sure,' said Williams. 'Dale's been at the window for ten minutes. We couldn't get at him. We'll have to stop trying, now.'

The men on the fire-escape came into view. They were signalling. Cunningham could not understand what they wanted, but assumed that they were telling Williams that the situation had become hopeless. Andrew Dale was up there in that inferno, helpless, waiting only for the end.

'What——' began Williams, and then a note of excitement sounded in his voice. 'They want to move—Lord love us, there he is!'

A man appeared on the roof of the next building. Cunningham did not recognise Andrew Dale, but Williams seemed to be in no doubt as to who it was. A tiny, crawling figure, Andrew was getting further away from the thick of the flames, but the building on to which he had climbed was itself catching alight.

The fire-escape moved slowly forward. The great ladder and the platform swayed sickeningly. It was miraculous that the men kept their hold. Soon, it stopped immediately in front of Andrews. Flames were on either side of him, and powerful jets of water were being sent on to the roof near him, keeping the flames at bay.

The platform swayed towards him as the men in charge below worked the mechanism. The firemen on the platform were doing something—throwing a rope. Andrew clutched at it, and missed. The second time he caught it and tied it about his waist. Then the platform seemed to touch the top of the house. After a tense moment Andrew stood swaying on the platform.

The crowd roared.

'Well, I wouldn't have believed it,' said Williams, delightedly. 'He's a lucky beggar! That wasn't far short of murder, Cunningham; you nearly had another one on your hands.'

Cunningham snapped: 'What do you mean?'

'I mean that this fire wasn't an accident,' said Williams, wiping the sweat off his forehead. 'We could smell the petrol when we first arrived, which was pretty early on. Five minutes after the first alarm to be exact, and by then the fire had already taken a firm hold. It's an old building, but it shouldn't have burned like that. It's arson all right.'

'Oh,' said Cunningham, and he felt a great relief at the knowledge that the man from Scotland Yard would soon be here.

He went towards the fire-escape.

Andrew Dale's clothes were scorched and his hair singed, but he had suffered little injury.

'I'm all right,' he insisted, 'but I would like a cup of tea.'

As he spoke, the manageress of the restaurant appeared, carrying a tea-tray. Andrew laughed.

'There couldn't be quicker service than that, could there?'

'No,' said Cunningham, who was standing near by. 'Are you feeling well enough to spare me a few minutes, Mr. Dale?'

'If you think it's necessary,' said Andrew tersely.

'It *is* necessary,' said Cunningham.

He knew he was being exacting, but the newspaperman, Lecky, was standing near by, and he did not want it known that arson was the cause of the fire. Andrew Dale would have to assume that he was wanted about his uncle's murder.

Lecky, looking about him, espied Cunningham, and came up jauntily.

'Hallo, Inspector! Anything new from the Chief Constable?'

Cunningham said shortly: 'No.'

'Well, don't forget to let me know when anything does turn up,' said Lecky. 'I say, that bookmaker, Porton's the name—is he coming back tomorrow?'

'I thought you knew everything,' said Cunningham, sarcastically.

'Oh no,' said Lecky, with a beaming smile. 'Not yet. Is it true there was a burglary at the Gantry's house tonight?' He kept his voice low, but that did not prevent Cunningham from being annoyed; the plump little man seemed to have an uncanny source of knowledge.

'Hadn't you better go and inquire?' he demanded.

'So there *was*,' said Lecky. 'Police lost their man. Too bad!' He winked, and turned away.

Andrew watched him thoughtfully.

'I suppose he *is* a reporter,' he said. 'He seems to pop up everywhere. He's tried three times to get a statement from me, and apparently he's been worrying you.'

'He's from the *Record*,' Cunningham said. 'I've checked that with the paper's local representative. He's a good man, I'm told.' He finished his tea. 'Ready?'

Andrew put down his cup, and together they walked to the police station, followed by a few stragglers from the crowd.

In Forrest's office, Andrew said: 'I hope you're not going to keep me long, Cunningham.'

'No longer than I can help,' Cunningham assured him. 'It's about the fire, Mr. Dale.'

'The *fire*? What about it?'

'Williams is sure it was arson,' said Cunningham, bluntly.

Andrew sat quite still. His face was set and his eyes were narrowed. It seemed a long time before he spoke.

'Is there no doubt at all?'

'I'm afraid not. Williams says he smelt the petrol.'

'It was certainly quick,' admitted Andrew. 'I was in my office when I first heard a shout outside, and saw flames shooting into the street. By the time I had collected a few important papers, the lower rooms were burning, that's why I made a dash for the stairs.' He fell silent again. Then abruptly: 'Why the devil should anyone want to set fire to the office?'

'I was hoping you could tell me that.'

'Well, I can't. There was nothing there at all unusual, but many valuable records have gone up in smoke. It's going to be a terrible job getting the business in order again.' Andrew leaned forward wearily. 'Have you any idea who started it?'

'None at all.'

'You've got your hands full, haven't you?' demanded Andrew. He laughed harshly. 'Is there anything else? I don't mind admitting that I'm just about all in.'

'No, I needn't worry you any more tonight. I'll have someone drive you home, if you like.'

'I'd be grateful,' Andrew said.

He sat looking straight ahead of him on the short journey to his house. Cunningham, who had after all driven him himself, did not ask further questions. They said goodnight, then Cunningham drove off. Andrew went indoors. The two servants were in bed, the house was in darkness. He passed his mother's door, and went along to his own room, opened the door and switched on the light—and found the place a shambles. Drawers had been emptied and their contents piled on the floor, the mattress had been taken off the bed and ripped open, pillows torn out of their cases. The pictures had been removed from the walls, and the carpet pulled up at two corners. He stood for a few seconds, staring at it: and then he turned stiffly and walked towards the telephone.

Cunningham was just about to leave the office when the telephone bell rang.

Jim Gantry was late in getting up the next morning. They had all sat up talking until long after midnight. George had certainly seemed a new man, and something of his vitality affected Marjorie, who became younger and more carefree. The thought of an entanglement with Andrew as the third party faded from Jim's mind. Angela, he decided, had probably been wrong; there was some other explanation of the tension which had affected the trio on the Langford's arrival.

He thought ruefully that there would be little work done that day. He was not particularly busy, but he could not afford to lose too much time. It would be difficult to concentrate while Paddy was in jail, but even if he were released, the mystery would remain, and make concentration difficult. The Langfords' arrival had created undreamed of complications.

Marjorie was downstairs, getting breakfast. She had been first up, roused by Tub, and had already made morning tea. It was good to think that she intended to pull her weight in the house.

Angela and Tub went downstairs. George tapped on Jim's door and asked if the bathroom were free.

'Yes, all clear. How are you this morning?'

'Oh, I'm all right.' His appearance certainly confirmed his words. 'I told you I should be,' he went on. 'Are you sure I won't be keeping anyone out?'

'Yes, quite sure,' said Jim.

As he went downstairs, the newspaper boy walked along the drive. Jim opened the door and waited for him. He liked to look through the *Daily Record* before breakfast while keeping *The Times* for more leisurely reading.

A front page headline read: ARSON FOLOWS MURDER, and the sub-heading ran: MALLING MYSTERY DEEPENS. Then he read the story.

What Lecky did not know, he had guessed with remarkable shrewdness. The story made graphic reading, and the account of Andrew Dale's narrow escape made Jim hold his breath. It was not until he reached the foot of the column that he read his own name:

Mr. James Gantry, the distinguished literary critic and biographer, employer of Paddy O'Hara, is convinced of his servant's innocence and will do everything in his power to establish it.

It went on to mention the burglary when the Langfords' luggage had been tampered with; how the man had obtained information about that was beyond Jim, but he read on. Lecky wrote that Jim and Dale were good friends and that the Langfords were staying with the Gantrys at least until the mystery was solved.

Angela called out: 'Jim, see if George is ready for breakfast.'

Jim nodded, and glanced at the paper again. His eye caught the *Stop Press*, and he drew in his breath. '*Another Malling Burglary*', he read, and underneath the brief report ran:

The home of Mr. Andrew Dale was burgled last night, at

66

the same time as Mr. Dale's offices were gutted by fire. See story on page 1.

Marjorie came out of the kitchen, wheeling a trolley.

'What's the matter, Jim?'

'Everything's the matter,' said Jim. 'Andrew's office was destroyed by fire last night.'

He continued the story over breakfast. Angela was agog, but Jim thought that while the girls were excited and shocked, and still talked about it while they cleared the table and went to wash-up, it was only George who was greatly worried.

Jim said: 'Care to come up to my study?'

'No, you're busy——' George hesitated.

'Not after this,' said Jim. He led the way up. 'I don't think either of them realises what it means, do you?'

'No,' said George, 'but someone is bound to tell them sooner or later that it was a cold-blooded attempt to kill Andrew. He was lucky to escape.'

Jim nodded.

'Well,' said George, 'Paddy wasn't mixed up in last night's affair. I should say that the case against him is getting weaker and weaker. And I don't mind admitting that I'm glad all of us were here together last night—we didn't go to bed until after the time of the fire, did we?'

'No,' said Jim. They reached the study, and George took an easy chair. Jim sat at his desk, where the morning post was waiting unopened. 'I remember hearing the fire-bell—Angela remarked on it, didn't she? I'm not so sure that we're all in the clear, though.'

'Oh? How's that?'

'Well, no one else can swear that we were all here until after midnight.'

'Police were watching us,' George pointed out, 'they'd be on their toes after the earlier mistake, don't you think? The very fact that the house was being watched will ensure that we don't come under suspicion for this particular crime.' He smiled in his slow, attractive fashion. 'You've come to accept the fact that you're under suspicion, haven't you?'

Jim shrugged. 'It's the only thing to do.'

'I suppose so. I can't get used to the idea myself. I suppose we ought to telephone Andrew.'

'I expect he'll be along this morning,' Jim said. 'He never worries except about important things, and our curiosity doesn't rate as important. If he isn't here by half-past ten, I think I'll go along and see Cunningham. Or,' he added, thoughtfully, 'I could try to find Lecky. He seems to know everything that happens.' He heard the front gate slam, and looked out casually. 'Well, talk of the devil—here *is* Lecky,' he exclaimed. 'I'll go down and let him in.'

Jim was filled with unaccountable excitement as he hurried down the stairs. Had Lecky come with good news? He felt sure that the man would not have come just for another chat. Lecky's smile, when Jim opened the front door, put an edge to his expectation, for the newspaperman looked in great good humour.

''Morning!' he greeted. 'Up with the lark, Gantry?'

'Hardly with the lark. What's brought you?'

'A herald of good tidings,' declared Lecky, cheerfully. 'I think you'll soon have O'Hara back with you.'

'*What?*'

'It's a fact,' said Lecky, as they went upstairs. 'What, *another* flight?'

'Yes, I work at the top of the house.'

'You ought to have a lift,' declared Lecky. 'It isn't human to walk up all these stairs. I'm surprised at you. This is an age of progress.' Introduced to George, he flopped down, assuming an air of utter exhaustion. 'Well, I'm not coming up here very often,' he declared. 'If you want to see me, it'll have to be on the ground floor.'

Jim said: 'All right, hint taken, but what's this about Paddy?'

'Good news,' declared Lecky. 'The burglary at Dale's house was the first real step forward. Ladder against the window, everything done in exactly the same fashion as the other burglaries. No fingerprints, no clues—except one. The burglar was a ginger-haired man.'

'What?' cried Jim.

Lecky grimaced at George. 'I didn't think Gantry would get excited so easily, did you? It's a fact, Gantry. You remember the policeman who thought he saw O'Hara climbing down the ladder from old Coombs's room just after the murder?'

'Yes.'

'The same policeman saw the same man climbing out of Andrew Dale's room last night. He gave chase but lost him. Apparently Dale surprised the fellow, who had to leave before he finished his job. I had a bit of luck,' went on Lecky, beaming. 'I followed Cunningham when Dale called him to the house and was around when this policeman, who thought he once saw O'Hara, turned up. They talked in a front room, and my ear was glued, as they say, to the window.' The little man's irrepressible good spirits were contagious, and they both laughed. 'So this morning, I looked in on Cunningham. He was a bit short-tempered, and I don't wonder at it. But he calmed down after telling me that if I snooped around any more he would boot me out of the town, and then admitted that I'd heard aright. The police cannot now identify O'Hara as the man who burgled Coombs's room. They've still got the evidence that O'Hara had a collection of loot in his room, and the forty-one pounds or whatever it was, but——' He paused, and looked expectantly at Jim.

Jim said: 'The policeman who identified Paddy first said he followed him here.'

'Exactly! But there's at least a chance that it wasn't Paddy at all but the other chap! If the fellow had a key and let himself in, he could have planted that pigskin wallet and the cash on Paddy. Now there's irrefutable evidence of two gingerheads being about, defending counsel would make hay of the police case. My opinion is that the police will release Paddy today, although they'll still keep an eye on him. That doesn't matter so much.'

'It certainly doesn't,' exclaimed Jim, warmly. 'You've taken a load off my mind!'

'Always glad to be of service,' observed Lecky. 'What were they after from your suitcases, Mr. Langford—any idea?'

'None at all.'

Lecky beamed. 'That's a pity. Between you and me, I think I know what it was. You won't breathe a word if I tell you?'

'No!' exclaimed George and Jim in unison.

'Coombs's will,' declared Lecky, loftily.

'His *will*?'

'Last will and testament,' continued Lecky. 'It might be important. It might even provide the motive for the murder. Let's assume that *someone* wants it. Supposing he thought you had it? What would he do but come to find out?'

George said slowly: 'I can't imagine why anyone would think *I* might have the will. I certainly haven't.'

'Oh, granted! But people get queer ideas.'

'What should I want it for?' asked George.

Lecky pretended to be nervous. 'Now don't throw things at me if I answer, will you? After all, your wife *is* old Coombs's next-of-kin, isn't she? If there's no will, then she will automatically inherit. Quite a motive. You can't say I don't take you into my confidence,' he added.

George said rather grimly: 'You certainly do that.'

The statement had distressed him. His smile had gone, and he looked bleak and troubled. Watching him, Jim was thinking of the cold logic of Lecky's statement, and forcing himself to realise what the reporter was implying—that George and Marjorie had the strongest possible motive for destroying the will if Marjorie were not a substantial legatee.

'Want more?' asked Lecky.

'Let it all come,' invited Jim.

'Well, you've *asked* for it. What happened next? The fire at the offices. Why? *Possibly* to try to make sure that the will was destroyed. A great number of documents must have been destroyed in that fire, you know. Coombs's office was on the ground floor. *The fire started from there.* There's incontrovertible proof—I've made a friend of the N.F.S. Captain. The room was soaked in petrol and then fired. Well, the seeker of the will must have considered there was a third possible hiding-place for it—Andrew Dale's room. So, he paid a visit there. If what I hear is right, he made a very thorough job of it, slit the mattress and tore open the pillows—that kind of thing. We don't know whether he found what he was after, of course. And I may be all wrong in my theories, but I thought you would like to know how the brain cells were working.'

'Yes,' said Jim. 'I'm very grateful.'

'Why have you told us, Mr. Lecky?' George asked.

'I'll ask a favour of you, one day,' said Lecky, 'and now I must be going. I want to have a nap before lunch, not having

70

had much sleep last night.' He glanced out of the window, and as he did so his smile widened and he clapped his hands together with a loud bang. 'Take your tips from Lecky!' he intoned. 'Never a loser, never a loser!'

Jim jumped up, and saw Paddy bounding up the drive. He also heard Tub's pattering footsteps as the child ran to meet him.

CHAPTER NINE

JOYOUS HOMECOMING

'I've never been so delighted in all me life,' cried Paddy, as Angela, Jim and Tub crowded round him. Marjorie and George stood a little way off, while Lecky grinned from the upstairs window. 'Begorrah, it was worth being locked up to tell the policemen what I thought of them, and they thinking I'd be dangling at the end of a rope before the year was out, the idiots.'

'Paddy!' cried Tub.

'It's your humble servant back, same as ever he was, with a soft spot in his wicked old heart for the likes of ye, ye lump of mischief that ye are! What's he been doing, Mrs. Gantry, while I've been away? Have ye been looking after him properly, now? Has he had his spoonful of honey night and morning?'

Angela laughed. 'Paddy, you've only been away a day!'

'Sure and it seemed the whole of me life,' declared Paddy. He looked up and saw George and Marjorie. 'Why, it's visitors we have, I see! Welcome ye are, and that's from the bottom of me heart and the heart of Paddy O'Hara is a deep one, but you won't need telling that. Have you got dinner on, Mrs. Gantry?'

'We are having cold lamb,' Angela said.

'Indeed we're not,' declared Paddy. 'Out of prison a man comes straight into your house and ye offer him cold lamb, so you do.' He took a brown-paper parcel from under his arm. 'Now you can guess what's in this parcel and you won't, not if you tried until Christmas; it's a miracle so it is, and birds so short in this one-eyed town. It was the little girl with the merry eyes, the one who's always making a pass at me. "Why, Mr. O'Hara," she said, "I thought ye were in prison."

"Prison," said I, "that's not for the likes of me, but I go there sometimes to give the poor, misguided policemen a piece of me mind, and it's a celebration I'm having at the house," I told her, "What have ye got to make it a day in a thousand?" "Nothing," said she. "Nothing!" said I, indignant I was, "nothing! Ye'd tell a man saved by two fine gentlemen from the gallows tree, nothing ye'd offer him, what about a nice chicken?" said I. "Chicken!" said she. "The only chicken we've got in is on order and not for the likes of you." And here's the chicken and a plumper one ye've never seen in your life,' cried Paddy. He snatched the paper off and held the bird high.

He did not stop talking for the rest of the morning.

Marjorie and Angela had taken Tub out shopping, and George and Jim sat in the study. The more Jim saw of Marjorie's husband, the more he liked him. That dry humour, the slow, considered speech, the unruffled calm, all appealed to him. True, it made George's outburst of the previous evening seem out of character; but he felt that something had happened between Marjorie and George to bring about the attack and therefore to make George feel useless and unwanted.

On reflection, he thought that there might be grounds for Angela's suspicions, but he was not at all sure that she was right.

He was too relieved over Paddy to worry very much.

Now and again he heard a burst of song from the kitchen, and invariably it made him smile. If Paddy were no longer suspected, it stood to reason that police suspicions of him and Angela had also been discarded. But at the back of his mind he felt that it was not quite so easy as that.

'Do you think they've decided they were wrong about Paddy, or do you think they're biding their time?' George asked.

'I fancy they're biding their time,' said Jim. 'Mind you, the case is nothing like so strong against him. This other ginger-haired man——' He paused.

'Deep thoughts passing through your mind?' asked George.

'Well, certainly unpleasant ones,' admitted Jim. 'The existence of the second man virtually proves that a deliberate attempt was made to frame Paddy, doesn't it?'

'I suppose so.'

'And indirectly, to frame me.'

'I should think Paddy was the one they were after,' said George, reassuringly. 'They wanted a scapegoat. Paddy just happened to be about the right build and the right colouring, so they picked on him.'

'But that leads to another queer thing,' said Jim. 'Before they could try to frame him, they would surely have to know him fairly well.'

'Presumably,' admitted George.

'But no one in Malling *does* know Paddy well, if we except Andrew, Angela and I.'

George said: 'I know of one other person who might come into it, and whom you've forgotten.'

'Who?'

'Porton, the bookmaker.'

'Oh,' said Jim. 'Yes, I'd forgotten him. Didn't Lecky say that Porton had gone to Newmarket for a few days and that no one had been able to get in touch with him?'

'He did,' said George. 'That's reasonable enough, too, but Porton might have decided that it was a good time to get away from Malling.' He smiled. 'We're only speculating, of course. And we're forgetting another thing.'

'What's that?'

'Whoever framed Paddy killed Coombs. There must have been a motive. As Lecky was careful to point out, Marjorie and I had a pretty strong one. He also pointed out that Andrew, who automatically becomes the senior partner in the business, had one too. That keeps it in the family.'

Jim smiled. 'I think you are worrying unduly about that. You know, George, I've a feeling that much more was stolen than the·wallet and a few pounds in cash. I wonder if Coombs had a lot of money or valuables in his room.'

'More speculation,' said George. 'I wish Andrew would turn up. You might telephone him at his home, I think.'

Jim spoke to a servant at the Dales' home. She told him that Andrew had been out since ten o'clock, and that she had no idea where he was.

'Supposing we go down into the town,' suggestd George. 'We might see something of him there.'

'I'll ring for a taxi,' said Jim. 'There isn't time to go by bus.'

A taxi arrived in ten minutes, and soon afterwards the two men reached the end of the High Street. The smell of burning was still strong, and two or three N.F.S. men were standing about. Jim was surprised at the extent of the damage.

A notice pinned to a board outside the shell of the offices read: *Dale, Coombs and Dale, Temporary Offices, 1a High Street, 1st Floor.*

'We'll try that,' said George.

1a High Street was on a corner. A large firm of clothiers tenanted the shop and the ground floor. The side entrance was narrow and there were several names pasted up on a notice board. They did not look at the board, but went slowly up the stairs. As they reached the landing, Jim noticed another name, in heavy black, with an arrow pointing towards the next flight of stairs. The name was: *Sam Porton, Commission Agent.*

'I wonder if Porton's back,' Jim remarked, as he tapped on the door of *Dale, Coombs and Dale's* temporary office. A girl called 'Come in.' She was the receptionist who had received Jim when he had last called on Andrew.

'I'm sorry, sir, Mr. Dale's out, and I don't know when he will be in,' she said in a rather flustered way. 'If you come back tomorrow morning you might be able to see him.'

'Thanks,' said Jim. They went out immediately. 'We're wasting our time,' he declared.

'I couldn't agree more,' said George. 'I——'

He broke off. A man's voice was coming from another room. Jim's first reaction was annoyance that Andrew had not come out to see them; for the voice was Andrew's all right.

'No, darling, I haven't the faintest idea of why it happened or what it's all about,' he was saying. 'If only I did! It wouldn't matter so much if it weren't for you and me. It—it's driving me mad.'

'Andrew, my dear!'

That was Marjorie's voice.

'It's true. I can't think. I can't collect myself. None of these other things really matter.'

Jim glanced at George. He was standing quite still, his face set, looking towards the door. There was nothing Jim could do

75

or say. He waited, with a sickening sense of uselessness, for Marjorie's next words.

'Andrew, we settled all that months ago, it's not fair to keep talking about it.'

'Fair! You know perfectly well that if he weren't a crook you would leave him right away. Why on earth did you marry him? Why didn't you realise what you were doing? For once in his life the Old Man was right——'

'Andrew, *please*!'

'We've got to do something about it,' Andrew declared hoarsely. 'I shan't be sane until it's settled. You're chained to a man who will never do a day's work in his life; surely you've done enough for him!'

Marjorie said: 'Unless you stop talking like this, Andrew, I shall go.'

There was a moment's silence. Jim wished he were anywhere but on that landing, wished that someone would come up the stairs and interrupt them, forcing the couple in the other office to realise that they could be overheard. But no one came, and after a long pause Andrew spoke again.

'I'm sorry, darling. It must be the excitement. First the Old Man, then the fire, then the burglary—and the terrible mess we're in. All our records gone, everything burned up, with a dozen urgent cases ready for the County Court.'

'I know it's difficult,' Marjorie said.

'I just can't see how I'm going to sort it out,' Andrew confessed. 'But you're right, of course. Whenever I can make myself look at things calmly, I realise that. Good old Marjorie, loyal to the core.' There was bitterness in his laugh. 'Well, there it is. How did you manage to get away this morning?'

'Angela and I came out shopping. Shoes for Tub. I'm meeting her at half-past twelve at the end of the High Street. What time is it now?'

'Ten past.'

'Then we've got twenty minutes. Andrew, we must talk about the murder. We *must*. I'm sure the police think that George and I know something about it.'

Andrew said: 'Darling, I refuse to consider nonsense of that kind. Whatever silly idea is buzzing about in the police bonnets we shall know before the day's out. Then we can talk about it. I'll come to the Gantrys, and we can discuss it with them. Don't let's waste the few moments we've got to ourselves in talking about the murder. You and I——'

Jim felt George's hand on his arm.

They went downstairs. George did not speak. A car drew up outside as they reached the street, but neither of them really noticed it. A short, fat man in a check suit got out. He had a pair of field-glasses slung over his shoulder. The chauffeur standing by the open door was holding a suitcase.

George said: 'I'll find my own way back.'

'The taxi's just along here,' said Jim.

'I'd rather find my own way——'

'Sorry,' said Jim. 'I don't trust you on your own.'

George looked him full in the eyes, and Jim saw, in the lean, handsome face, the drawn lips and the eyes which seemed to burn and suffer, how deep the hurt had gone.

In silence they walked towards the taxi. George must have a little while on his own, Jim decided, to get over the shock of those revelations. Yet ought he to be left alone, even in the house? The thought of suicide was already in his mind.

Outside the house, Jim paid off the cabby.

George said: 'All right, Jim. I won't act the fool.'

'I wish I could trust you,' Jim said.

'You can, though I could give you twenty logical reasons why I would be wiser and kinder to kill myself.'

He put out a hand and rested it against a tree.

'The only other way out is divorce,' he went on, 'but I don't believe that Marjorie would agree to it. She would if I were well, but she won't because I'm what I am.'

Jim said abruptly: 'Was it a surprise to you?'

'No. I've had an idea of what they felt for some time, but I wasn't certain until now.'

'You've stuck it so far,' said Jim, 'surely you can go on?'

'It's easy to say that,' George retorted, 'not quite so easy to carry it out.'

Jim said: 'I know I'm an outsider and I've no right to interfere, but as long as you're staying here, Gorge, you're under my protection. I can't stop you leaving, but I hope you'll stay and I hope you'll give this thing a chance to work out, because one thing is obvious to me although it may not be

77

to you.'

'What's that?'

'Marjorie loves you at least as much as she loves him,' said Jim, 'and probably better. This other could burn itself out. Why not wait and see.'

As they went into the hall, they met Paddy coming out of the dining-room. He looked hot and happy, and told them the bird was done to a turn. He hoped Mrs. Gantry's friend wouldn't keep her out too long. Then off he went, and there was genuine amusement in George's smile.

'You're lucky in having Paddy,' he said.

The others arrived soon afterwards. There was no hint of embarrassment in Marjorie's manner, and George played up well. Jim wondered if he would be wise to tell Angela what had happened. If he did so, there was the chance that she might take it on herself to reproach Marjorie, and that would only complicate a bad situation. He decided to say nothing, at least until that night.

Now and again, as the day wore on, he wondered whether he could trust George to keep his word.

He tried not to think about it.

Cunningham had a telephone message immediately after lunch, telling him to expect Maitland at half-past four. Probably Maitland would have the Scotland Yard man with him, he thought. Cunningham still felt relieved by that decision, for the morning had yielded nothing but a further welter of complications. Cunningham managed only to be certain on one point: the murder, the fire and the burglary at the Gantrys' house and at Dale's house were connected. He was not now sure that the earlier series of burglaries was connected with the murder, although he thought it likely.

Owen was still watching the Gantrys' house, and had already reported the joyous homecoming. Both men admitted that Paddy O'Hara behaved very unlike a murderer; it was hardly possible to believe that he had murder on his conscience. Once he was sure that another man had been mistaken for him, Cunningham had released him, although Paddy refused to say where he had got the stolen clothes. Cunningham put his refusal down to obstinacy strengthened by resentment.

78

Owen would watch Paddy closely, and there was little likelihood of another slip, for the curly-haired sergeant was still smarting after his failure.

Just before half-past four Maitland came in with a large man, an exceedingly bulky man, swaying forward on small, exquisitely-shod feet. With a sinking heart Cunningham realised that he must be the man from Scotland Yard. A flash of recognition crossed his mind. He did not so much know him, as know of him. A man with a strong appetite for fame and food—of the recherché kind—and a still stronger one for results. Cunningham's heart sunk still lower as he reviewed the humiliating lack of anything whatever in this case that he could present under such a designation.

Maitland, after introducing Superintendent Folly, went on easily: 'I am not going to stay, Cunningham, except to hear anything fresh that has developed.'

'I hope you'll approve of what I've done, sir,' said Cunningham, a trifle desperately. 'I've released O'Hara.' He expected a shocked exclamation, but neither Maitland nor Folly spoke.

Very slightly, Cunningham's spirits rose.

'Well, yes,' Maitland said at last. 'It would seem to be the only thing to do. Is the bookmaker back yet, do you know?'

'He arrived a little after twelve o'clock,' Cunningham told him. 'I saw him at half-past twelve, sir. He has taken bets with O'Hara, and he's got records of them. He's promised to have a full report ready for this evening.'

'Right.' Maitland rose with a certain alacrity. 'Then I'll leave the two of you to get to know each other. Goodnight.'

Cunningham got up to open the door, then closed it on the Chief Constable and turned to look at Folly. For a moment a certain gleam of—sardonic amusement?—showed in the Superintendent's eyes. But Cunningham preferred not to see it, concentrating rather on the benignly smiling lips.

'You've picked one out for me, haven't you?' he demanded.

Cunningham laughed in relief. 'It's certainly a teaser. It isn't that there aren't any clues, but that there are so many.'

Folly spread his hands.

'Before we start, could we perhaps indulge in a little tea? And maybe a biscuit or two. Digestive preferably, but we will not cavil at petit beurre. Fortified, much may be attempted;

79

unfortified——' Folly shrugged eloquently.

A little taken aback—for was this *mountebankery* (a strong word, but surely justified) real, or feigned—Cunningham sent an order down to the canteen.

Humming a little tune, Folly waited for the tray, receiving it with tranquil enjoyment. Not until the last biscuit crumb had been airily flipped away from the Superintendent's irreproachable lapel, did he turn back to the desk.

'Ah-h. Never neglect the inner man, Cunningham. What were you saying?'

Methodically Cunningham recapitulated the case. At the end of an hour his distrust had turned to almost enthusiasm. Folly's shrewd comments were sharp and very much to the point.

'There's no sign of the will yet?'

'None at all.'

'And the origin of the fire?'

Cunningham shook his head.

'No luck there either. There's an alleyway at the back of the shops, and in the yard of *Dale, Coombs and Dale* there was a garage where old Coombs and Dale kept their cars. Both were burnt out. Petrol was always kept there, so it's reasonable to assume that someone who knew of this probably started the fire. The whole staff of the firm, the garage people, tradesmen, all knew about it, so it doesn't help very much.'

'Names and addresses?'

'Oh yes. They've all been questioned. Or are being. That's how the *Record* man Lecky got on to it.'

Folly gave a high-pitched whinnying laugh.

'I know the chappie you mean. He's all right.'

'He's made a nuisance of himself,' Cunningham grumbled. 'He even went to the Gantrys' house this morning, just before O'Hara was released. The man's uncanny.'

'He gets around,' said Folly. 'I shouldn't worry about Lecky, if I were you. Now, I'm rather intrigued by this emotional mix-up between Andrew Dale and the Langfords. I have got this clear, haven't I?—Marjorie Langford is the niece and only close relative of Coombs, and she married Langford against her uncle's wish. Coombs thereafter refused to help them except on pretty harsh terms. Coombs insisted on

80

a repayment of the debt, Andrew Dale took her side, and that caused the quarrel.'

'That's all true,' said Cunningham.

'Langford himself knew nothing about the quarrel?'

'Well, he wasn't there,' said Cunningham. 'He was at Dale's home.'

'Let me get this straight,' said Folly, playing in a rather annoying way with a silver pencil. '*Mrs.* Dale is a widow. Her son lives at home. He is not engaged, has never been a ladies' man. The Langfords were staying with the Dales, whose house is a few doors away from Mr. Coombs's. There was some feeling between Mrs. Dale and Marjorie Langford. As a result, as far as you have found out, the Langfords left and went to the Gantrys'.'

'That's right.'

'You had no idea of the reason for the trouble between the two women, but this morning you had a report about a talk between Andrew Dale and Marjorie Langford, which suggests that they are having an *affaire*. If Mrs. Dale, who is a puritannical old lady, knew that her son and a married woman were seeing too much of each other, she might have made trouble.'

'She *is* pretty narrow,' admitted Cunningham.

'That seems to be the explanation then,' said Folly. He had tired of the pencil, dropping it with a certain petulance. 'Old Coombs was against this marriage from the first, and made difficulties. Nevertheless his money will go to the Langfords of whom he disapproved so plainly, if the will doesn't turn up. Either Marjorie or George Langford could have committed the murder with that end in mind—or Dale could have committed it, with a view to getting complete control of the business.'

Cunningham said: 'If the murder were committed by the man who started the fire, that cuts Dale out, for he would hardly try to get control of the business and then destroy it.'

'That's reasonable,' admitted Folly magnanimously.

'And it seems to narrow it down to the Langfords and the ginger-haired man. He might be working for them.'

But this Folly would not allow.

'Come, come. It's a pretty cold-blooded thing to hire an

81

assassin, you know. The Langfords might take violent action owing to a quarrel—a sudden flare up, but this was planned, premeditated. Hardly in their line, surely?'

Shaken, but determined not to let Folly have it all his own way, Cunningham asserted doggedly:

'I wouldn't go as far as that. If the Langfords knew that they would benefit by Coombs's death, they might have planned this some time ago.'

Folly smiled impishly.

'Oh, we mustn't write that off entirely. But the Langfords are pretty hard up, aren't they?'

'So I hear.' Caution tinged Cunningham's voice. He had no intention of being led on to say something that Folly would then blandly flatten.

'And a man such as this red-haired fellow wouldn't commit murder on the mere *chance* of getting a reward,' said Folly. 'He would want cash on the nail, and that, we can assume, the Langfords could not produce. No, my dear chap, I don't think there is any evidence that the Langfords employed the red-haired man. You're wrong there. Mrs. Langford went back to her husband at the Dales' house after the quarrel with Coombs, I believe.'

'Yes.'

'And Dale returned to the house rather later, but both of them certainly left Coombs alive, because after they left he spoke to his servant.'

'That's right,' said Cunningham, for surely he couldn't go wrong in agreeing with the Superintendent.

Folly looked at him reproachfully.

'But is it? What about the Langfords' movements after that?' He beamed suddenly. 'Could either or both of them have made a second visit to Coombs's home, killed him and got back?'

Made reckless by adversity Cunningham said a trifle wildly: 'I suppose they could have. So could Andrew Dale. But surely it's pretty certain that the red-haired man committed the murder.'

Folly said gently: 'No, I don't think so.'

'But——'

Folly said with the kindly testiness of one instructing the

young: 'Think, my dear chap, think. Because you're so close to it, Cunningham, you've missed one or two possibilities. First, the burglar might have paid his visit, stolen the money and got away, leaving Coombs asleep but unhurt. Second, he might have paid his visit, found Coombs dead, snatched the wallet and made his getaway. There has been this series of burglaries, remember. The man's visit might have been in the way of ordinary business, and the murder coincidental. Coombs was the kind of man who might be worth a visit. I certainly shouldn't rule out coincidence, would you?'

'I suppose not,' admitted Cunningham, a trifle bitterly. 'Well, I'm having the town combed for ginger-haired men—I seem to have been doing that for weeks!—and I think another visit to O'Hara is called for. He refused to say where he bought his dressing-gown and the other things, you know. I wonder if it would be a good idea to go and see him now?'

Folly leapt up with almost a bound. For such a large man he was remarkably nimble. The desk shook, the pencil rolled, but both were stabilised in an instant by Folly's pink hand. It was a plump, almost girlish hand, and far too well-fed, thought Cunningham, gloomily assessing it and not knowing whether to approve or disapprove, but there was strength in it.

He led the way downstairs. His car was waiting outside. The crowd was still gaping at the blackened ruins of the solicitor's office, and the firemen were still working among the debris.

Ten minutes later they pulled up near the Gantrys' house. Owen came forward, his hair stirred by a stiff breeze.

'Are they all in?' asked Cunningham.

'All except the child, who's at a party along the street,' Owen told him, 'and Andrew Dale's there, too. He arrived about a quarter of an hour ago.'

Folly was already striding up the drive at such a spanking pace that the two younger men, meekly following, were forced into an undignified trot.

CHAPTER TEN

ALL TOGETHER

It had been an uncomfortable quarter of an hour for Jim. Outwardly, however, George was unaffected by Andrew's presence. Marjorie was as cheerful as usual, but Andrew looked tired out. Some idea of the burden which weighed so heavily on him showed in his face, in the way he slumped back in his chair, in the moments when he closed his eyes, as if he could not rest them enough.

Jim, wishing he would go, looked out of the window and saw Cunningham and a stranger walking up the drive.

'Hallo,' he said. 'Police.'

No one made any comment except Angela, who said irritably that she wished they'd leave them alone. Now that Paddy had been released there was no excuse at all for all this badgering.

When Folly came in the room however, they looked up with the interest unconsciously paid to a personality.

'How can we help you?' Jim asked.

Folly gave a low and somewhat theatrical bow.

'I'm afraid we're going to worry an old bone,' he said, blandly taking command. 'There is one small thing which hasn't been satisfactorily explained yet, Mr. Gantry.' He spread his hands.

'What is it?'

'Where O'Hara bought his dressing-gown and various items of apparel.' Folly's voice was gentle, misleadingly apologetic. 'He refused to give the name of the person or the shop where he bought them. Has he told you?'

Jim said: 'No. But then, I've never asked him.'

'Most understanding, but hardly helpful.'

Jim said thoughtfully: 'I think you've missed one thing

about him. He's bitterly angry with the police.'

'Ah, very interesting. And this bitter anger is waged on the police as a whole, or in part?'

Jim looked at Folly sharply—was he being laughed at? He said, a little imperiously: 'He resents the way he was taken straight off to the police station without being given any opportunity to send a message. By acting like that, you made him obstinate, I'm afraid. His attitude is simply this: "they think they're so clever, let them find out what they want without worrying me." In a man like Paddy, that's understandable.'

Jim wished it didn't sound so childish. The childishness was confirmed by Folly's smile.

'You mean you think it would be unwise for us to question him tonight.'

'I do,' admitted Jim. 'Please yourself, of course. I'll send for him, if you like, or you can go and see him in the kitchen.'

'I think we'll have him in here.'

'I'll go and get him.' Jim got up.

'Do you mind if I come with you?' Folly's voice could not have been more suave or gentle, but Jim was beginning to feel a little out of his depth. He expected to lead the conversation, and he was not doing so. Truculence he could have combated, even hidebound authority, but the strength of Folly seemed to strike without visible weapons. A laughable man, and yet one could not laugh.

One thing was evident: the police thought that Paddy refused to divulge the name of the supplier because he was protecting that supplier; and such an attitude would immediately bring him and Angela back into the limelight.

They found him sitting on the kitchen table drinking a cup of strong tea.

'What, more visitors, Mr. Gantry? It's a day for them! Good afternoon, sir.'

'Good afternoon, Mr. O'Hara,' said Folly courteously. 'You look as if you have been very busy.'

'Sure and I've been busy,' declared Paddy, emphatically. 'Nearly twenty-four hours of my life has been stolen from me, and Mr. Gantry will bear me out on that; it's starved they were while I was away.' He rushed forward, pulled open the oven door and grabbed an oven-cloth. Two pies were revealed. 'It's burnt they would have been if I'd waited another minute,' he declared. 'I'm apologising for speaking so sharply, sir, but it was urgent, you'll admit.'

Folly's eye glistened.

'Ah ha, Mr. O'Hara, it's a fine cook you are! Never, since I won the favour of a master chef in the South of France, have I seen such pies! No doubt they taste as delicious as they look.'

Over O'Hara's face spread an expression that could only be termed a smile.

'And well ye might say so, sir, I vouch that . . .'

'Paddy——' began Jim, desperately.

'Mr. Gantry is trying to tell you that I am a policeman,' said Folly gently.

There was complete silence, which Jim expected to be broken at any moment by a burst of Irish fury. Instead, Paddy screwed up his eyes and his mouth, looking first at Jim and then at Folly: and then suddenly gave a loud hoot of laughter.

'I'd be ashamed, that I should, coming here without a uniform or a breath of suspicion, buttering me up over me cooking and all! What is it you want to know?'

'I wasn't buttering you up over your cooking,' said Folly simply. 'I meant it. But what I came about was to ask you where you bought your dressing-gown.'

Paddy said sulkily: 'You're so clever, you can find out.'

'Mr. O'Hara——'

'Politeness will not serve to get an answer out of me,' declared Paddy, 'plain O'Hara it was in the police station, and not so polite at that. You can find out for yourself.'

'Paddy, you may make difficulties for yourself if you don't answer,' Jim remonstrated.

'Then I'll make them,' declared Paddy.

'And difficulties for Mrs. Gantry and me,' added Jim. 'Please tell them, Paddy.'

Paddy looked at him reproachfully.

'So ye'd help him find out what he ought to be clever enough to know,' he said. 'Well, so be it, Mr. Gantry, but I'll admit I'm disappointed in ye.' He waited a full minute, savouring his power and Folly's expectancy with keen relish. Then, anger vanished, he winked. ' 'Twas in the market-place.'

86

'Malling Market?' asked Folly.

'And what other market would I be going to?' demanded Paddy. 'It was there I came across a man who offered me a pair of boots that fitted me, so they did. So I bought them. Every Tuesday he was there, and that's where I bought my rightful property which I'll thank ye to return.'

'They were stolen goods,' Folly informed him.

'I've only your word for that,' said Paddy, scornfully.

'Well, I'll see what I can do, O'Hara. Did you buy them from a man with a stall?'

'Och, no, he had no stall, just a few oddments spread about him, with one or two of his best things in his hands, so they were.'

'Was he always in the same place?'

'Next to the cooked meats and pastry stall,' said Paddy importantly. He was in great good humour again.

'And what was this man like, O'Hara?'

'He was just a man,' said Paddy.

'Short or tall?'

'When I come to think of it, he wasn't so very much different in size from myself,' said Paddy, 'and the reason I took to him was the colour of his hair, which is the colour of mine. When I first went to him I thought he was from old Ireland, but mistaken I was.'

'A man with red hair,' murmured Folly.

Paddy flared up. 'Indeed my hair isn't red! It's a fine bright colour. Auburn's the word.'

'It is indeed,' said Folly heartily. 'I was referring to the man in the market.'

Mollified but suspicious, Paddy looked at Folly doubtfully.

'And the man's name?'

'I wouldn't be knowing.'

'Didn't you call him anything?'

Paddy grinned. 'What I called him is no business of yours! Sure, you can go to the market on Tuesday and see him for yourself, if ye haven't been fool enough to frighten him away with all the silly things ye've put into the newspaper.' Paddy turned a closer attention to his pastry board, and Folly took the hint.

In the hall, Jim said, a trifle defensively: 'I told you

87

O'Hara was quite a character, didn't I?'

'You certainly did,' Folly answered drily. 'The trouble is that being a character, like being a fool, can be an excellent cover.'

They joined the others. Jim noted that George and Andrew watched the Scotland Yard men closely. He wondered whether Andrew's bleak expression was caused by fatigue, or love of Marjorie, or whether there was something else that was worrying him.

Few men could have had more anxieties thrust upon them in so short a time.

Folly waved a plump white hand languidly in the air.

'Thanks very much for your help, Mr. Gantry. We shall probably want to see O'Hara again, to identify the man.'

'Of course,' said Jim. 'Will you let me know if this other fellow has been seen on the market?'

'Yes,' Folly promised.

Andrew asked if the policemen could give him a lift; Folly agreed without hesitation and Andrew went off, haggard and on edge. The four who remained stood in the window, watching him. George glanced at Marjorie. Her face was expressionless, except for a slight frown; was her heart aching for Andrew Dale?

Tub was brought home soon afterwards, and Marjorie and Angela went upstairs to put him to bed. George said that he thought he would like a walk. He went out, leaving Jim in the study trying to concentrate on a biography of Dickens which he was reviewing. It was no good. He put down his pen and stared out of the window. Would George come back? What would Marjorie do if he didn't? And what about Andrew—he had looked ill, almost desperate; he, too, might do something silly.

George returned after three-quarters of an hour, and before they went in to supper, the telephone rang. It was Cunningham.

'I thought you would like to know, Mr. Gantry, that Porton confirms the winning bets which O'Hara laid with him, on the days O'Hara has given us, and that the man with red hair is known to have a stand near the cooked meat stall in the market.'

Jim's heart leapt. 'Oh, that's splendid!'

'I thought you would think so,' said Cunningham drily. 'Goodbye.'

The news brightened the evening meal. Paddy simply snorted and said that the fools should have believed him in the first place, but there was no doubt in the onlookers' minds, as they watched him light-heartedly dashing back and forth to the kitchen, of his relief. Had the Langfords not been there, Jim would have thought the whole affair over and done with; but now he was weighed down by the apparently insoluble problem which faced George and Marjorie.

The Langfords were in their room when a car pulled up outside and a woman climbed out.

Angela said: 'Who on earth is that?'

As she walked briskly to the front door and rang the bell twice in quick succession, they noted that she was tall, angular and well-dressed.

Jim said doubtfully: 'I *think* it's Mrs. Dale.'

'*Andrew's* mother? What on earth are we to do? Why has she come here? It can't be to see Marjorie. Listen, she's ringing again. Where's Paddy?'

'Out in the back garden. He can't hear,' said Jim. 'I'll go.' He hurried out and his disquiet was not eased when he met Mrs. Dale's cold and antagonistic glance. He had seen her only once before, in Andrew's office, when her expression had been much the same as it was now.

'I understand that Mrs. Langford is here,' she said. 'I wish to see her.'

CHAPTER ELEVEN

TROUBLE-MAKER

She means trouble, thought Jim. His dislike of the woman, born at the instant, deepened. He became evasive.

'I don't know whether she is in.'

'Will you kindly find out?'

There was nothing for it but to let her in. He stepped aside, then showed her into the morning room, a somewhat bleak room rarely used.

Angela was waiting in the sitting-room.

'What does she want?'

'To see Marjorie.'

'What about?'

'She didn't say.'

'She's a trouble-maker if ever there was one,' said Angela. 'I gathered from Majorie that she made her life an absolute burden when she and George were staying with her. It wouldn't surprise me if Mrs. Dale and old Coombs *wanted* Marjorie to leave George, get a divorce, and marry Andrew. That's exactly what it looks like to *me*.'

'*Hush!*' urged Jim. 'You're talking too loudly. And we must tell Marjorie.'

'Well, that's what *I* think,' repeated Angela. She looked malevolently towards the morning-room door. 'I wouldn't mind telling her so, either. All right, darling, I'll tell Marjorie! You keep out of the old dragon's way.'

Marjorie was on the landing. Jim heard Angela talking to her, and soon gathered that Marjorie had no desire to come down and see Mrs. Dale. That did not surprise him, but it made him uneasy. Angela appeared to be trying to persuade her. The conversation dragged on, and then Marjorie said in a clearer voice:

'Yes, you're right, dear. I'll come down in a moment.'

A door opened and closed, and Angela came towards the head of the stairs. A moment later the door opened again and Marjorie called in a low-pitched voice:

'I can't come. George is ill again.'

'Ill!' exclaimed Angela.

Jim hardly knew why the news affected him as it did. He ran up the stairs immediately, filled with a great sense of disquiet. Marjorie was bending over George, who was lying on the bed. His limbs were shaking. He seemed worse than on the first occasion. His colour was deathly, his eyes glazed.

Jim said: 'Let me help.'

'You can't do anything——' Marjorie began.

Jim took one of George's hands. It was clenched tightly, the nails biting into the flesh. Jim prised it open, then opened his other hand and gripped that too. He glanced quickly at Marjorie.

'Get him something hot. That's the procedure, isn't it?'

Marjorie said: 'Yes. But this isn't like——'

Her voice tapered off. She turned and hurried out, with Angela at her heels.

Jim bent low, holding George's hands. Marjorie was right, this wasn't like the previous attack. But presently the pressure of the other's fingers relaxed, and he grew still. The paroxysm had lasted no more than five minutes. Now George was bathed in sweat. It was streaming down his forehead to the pillow, soaking his collar.

The girls came back, Angela carrying a tray.

Jim helped George to sit up. He looked absolutely exhausted. Marjorie held a cup of tea to his lips and he sipped awkwardly. Jim watched Marjorie. She was giving her whole mind to her husband. There was something in her manner which made Jim feel that he had been right when he had told George, earlier in the day, that Marjorie was in love with *him*, whatever her feelings were towards Andrew. If old Coombs and Mrs. Dale were trying to break up that marriage, it was the Devil's own work.

Great Scott! Mrs. Dale was still waiting downstairs.

Marjorie had also remembered.

'I can't see her now,' she said impatiently. She bent over her husband once again.

It was obvious that the worst of the attack was over, and Jim was not needed in the room. He went out, closing the door behind him, moving slowly down the stairs as he tried to get his thoughts in order. The attack *had* been different and that meant one of two things: either George was getting worse, *or* he had been poisoned, by his own hand or that of another.

Jim reached the hall as the morning-room door opened and Mrs. Dale stood on the threshold.

'I am surprised at such discourtesy,' she began. 'Will you please be good enough to tell Mrs. Langford that I am waiting?'

Jim said: 'She will not be able to see you, Mrs. Dale.'

'I insist——'

The woman's manner broke his self-restraint.

'You can't insist on anything! Mr. Langford has been taken ill, Mrs. Langford will be with him for some time, and it will not be convenient for you to wait.' He led the way firmly towards the front door, surprised at his own vehemence.

Mrs. Dale followed him. At the door, she paused.

'I hope you will be good enough to tell Mrs. Langford that I called and that I wish to see her as soon as possible.'

'I will,' Jim promised. He watched her as she drove away.

There had been something unreal about the whole episode, and as the taxi gathered speed, Jim knew that he had handled it badly and been unpardonably rude. This business was getting under his skin. Now, too, he was haunted by the possibility that George had taken poison. He wondered if the wise thing would be to call a doctor. It might seem unnecessary now that the attack was over; yet it would be satisfying to know the real cause of the attack.

He walked along the drive. At the gates, he saw Sergeant Owen lurking near. So the police were still on duty, and presumably there was a man at the back of the house as well as the front. The feeling of always being watched was disturbing.

Owen walked towards him.

'Good evening, sir. Is everything all right?'

'What makes you think it might not be?' asked Jim, sharply.

'Merely a routine question, sir.'

'Do you think this routine is necessary, now that O'Hara is

virtually cleared?' asked Jim.

'That is not for me to say, sir. I am obeying orders.'

Jim grunted, and turned away.

He rather liked the curly-haired policeman. He rather liked Cunningham, too, but it was disturbing to learn that suspicion of Paddy or himself still lingered in the minds of authority.

He was halfway along the drive when he heard a shout. He recognised Paddy's voice. The cry came from the back of the house, and contained a note of urgency and alarm. Jim broke into a run, Owen close behind him. Rounding the house, he saw an astonishing sight. Paddy was standing on the kitchen window-sill, his hands raised, *shouting at a man who was perched on the window-sill of the room above.*

The man was a stranger. Small, dark-haired, he was looking desperately about him.

Owen drew up.

'It looks as if we've got him *this* time,' he said with satisfaction. 'I——'

He broke off, for the man above had climbed back through the window.

Jim shouted: 'Watch the other side of the house, Owen!' He himself went to the front, determined that the man who had broken in should not get away. As Jim reached the front door, Angela came hurrying down the stairs.

'What on earth's the matter, Jim? What's all this shouting about?'

'There's a man upstairs,' Jim said, breathlessly.

Owen called out: 'We're watching both sides, sir, I've told O'Hara to stay at the back. Will you telephone the police station and tell them what's happening?'

'All right!' answered Jim. He put a hand on Angela's shoulder. 'Stay out here, sweet, and yell if the fellow appears at any of the windows.'

Angela rather nervously nodded agreement.

Jim made for the telephone which was near the front door. He had actually touched it when he heard footsteps on the landing above and saw the dark-haired man rushing towards the stairs. The man reached the top step, gripped the banister rail and swung himself over. He dropped lightly.

Was he going to make for the back door or the front?

93

Jim moved forward silently. The man was crouching against the staircase. The thin, foxy face was printed indelibly on Jim's mind, and he noticed that the black hair was shiny with oil. The intruder turned, as if to go towards the back door, then grabbed a chair and flung it at Jim.

Taken completely by surprise, Jim tried to dodge, but a leg of the chair struck him on the shoulder and sent him reeling. The black-haired man ran towards the front door. Jim tried to grab him but he was still off his balance, and went down as the intruder pushed him aside. Desperately, Jim struggled to get up again, and saw the man disappearing on to the drive.

'Angela!' Jim shouted. 'Angela, look out!'

Angela screamed!

Jim got to his feet and staggered to the door. He could not move quickly, but his mind was clear enough. He saw Angela standing in the middle of the drive, a stick in her hand. The black-haired man was running towards her. Footsteps at the side of the house suggested that Owen and the other policeman were hurrying to Angela's assistance.

The dark-haired man swerved. Angela flung the stick, not at his head but at his legs. It tripped him up, and he crashed down.

'Grand work!' gasped Jim.

But the man was up in a moment, and Angela rushed towards him, without thought of her own safety. He struck at her savagely, sending her staggering back. Then he ran on, with Owen in close pursuit and a heavily-built man in plain clothes several yards behind. Their quarry reached the gate two yards ahead of Owen, and turned right.

Jim went to Angela.

'I'm all right,' she gasped, 'go after him. Those fools will lose him!'

Jim obeyed her, but was too breathless to make much speed. When he reached the gate he saw the dark-haired man near the end of the road, Owen still a couple of yards behind him and the second policeman hopelessly out-distanced. It looked as if the intruder would get away.

Then Owen threw himself forward in a tackle. He brought his quarry down, and when Jim reached them Owen was smiling with satisfaction, the dark-haired man sitting dazedly on the kerb.

'Well, that was a close thing,' Owen said. 'It was very plucky of Mrs. Gantry, sir. I hope she's all right.'

'She is,' said Jim. 'Do you know this fellow?'

'No,' said Owen, 'but we soon will! I'll flag this car.'

The car was already travelling slowly, and the driver stopped at once.

'I'll see that you know what the fellow says as soon as possible,' Owen added. 'It'll be a help if you'll check up that nothing's missing, sir.'

As he spoke, the dark-haired man leapt to his feet, drove a punch to the policeman's stomach and dived into the car. The driver accelerated. The car shot forward, gathering speed. It all happened in a few seconds.

In a sudden rush of anger, Jim snapped: 'We seem to have made a complete mess of it.'

'The number!' cried Owen. 'What's the number?' He stood staring at the car. 'A-X-O-2——'

The car swung round a corner and disappeared.

A very subdued Sergeant Owen tapped on the door of Forrest's office and, at Cunningham's 'Come in,' stepped inside. Folly was standing by the desk and Cunningham was sitting with a pencil in his hand and a sheaf of papers in front of him. Both looked round.

'Hallo, Reg,' said Cunningham, unsuspectingly. 'I didn't realise you were to be relieved so early.'

'I'm not,' said Owen, gruffly. 'I've come a worse cropper than I did before.'

The others eyed him in silence, Cunningham in some alarm. Owen's face reflected his mortification, but it was not a moment to feel sorry for him. Folly's eyes narrowed.

At least, Cunningham said: 'What do you mean?'

'I actually had the fellow,' Owen said. 'I actually had my hands on him, I thought...'

He explained in some detail. Cunningham's dismay increased, but Folly seemed disinclined to be censorious.

'The car trick beat you,' he said, generously, 'and that's not surprising. I remember once—but that, though exceedingly interesting, is another story, and will go in my memoirs. Did you get the number?'

'Part of it,' said Owen. 'I've told them downstairs to put a call out for a Wolseley AXO2-plus. I didn't even get a good look at the driver. I can't tell you how ashamed I am,' he added. 'You'd better take me off this job; I'm worse than useless.'

'Now, steady,' said Folly, laying a kindly hand on Owen's arm. 'We all make mistakes—or some of us. Even *I*—what did Gantry say?'

'No more than I deserved,' muttered Owen. 'I doubt whether I would have got the fellow at all if it hadn't been for Mrs. Gantry. She's full of pluck, and far more sensible than her husband.'

Folly said: 'We'll go along and see Gantry, Cunningham. If it takes too long, no doubt we can get a meal at the nearest pub. Risky, of course, but I think I can distinguish between a fresh sausage roll and a stale one before much harm is done. But needs must, dear boys, needs must. You'd better come along, too, Owen.'

With remarkable speed Folly inserted his bulk into the front seat of the police car.

'Thank God he's not at the wheel!' prayed Cunningham in heartfelt thankfulness, for more than a few soul-scaring legends were afloat as to the Superintendent's driving.

They were soon in the sitting-room of the house in Bligh Avenue. Jim, Angela and Marjorie were present, George being still too ill to appear. Jim told his part of the story and gave a full description of the burglar, which tallied with Owen's. Angela confirmed it. Suavely, and with much waving of pink palms, Folly congratulated them both, giving Angela a special word of praise.

'Is anything missing?' he asked.

'Nothing at all, as far as I can find out,' said Jim, 'but I don't think the fellow had much chance to look round. Paddy spotted him. You'd like a word with him, wouldn't you?'

'Please.'

Paddy was found taking it easy in a somewhat dilapidated basket chair, a copy of *Racing Special* in his hands.

'It's them policemen, I suppose,' he declared morosely, his former truculence warring with a keen desire to be once again in the limelight.

'Well, yes, it is,' admitted Jim. 'They want to know when you saw the man at the window.'

Strongly protesting that it was only for the Gantrys' sake, and no one and nothing else on this earth would have got him to speak to the villains again, so help him, Paddy followed Jim back to the sitting-room.

Once there, he launched into his narrative.

'Sure and it's easy,' he declared. 'I was working on the potato patch, and cruel hard it is on your back, when straightening up to shift a plug of baccy out of me pocket, what should I see but this good-for-nothing climbing up the wall of the house. So I gave a shout to call Mr. Owen and his friends, and thankful I was that they were so close to hand, for I didn't at all like the look of the fellow at the window. And after him I went, but he trod on me hand and there's the truth of it. So I shouted again and Mr. Gantry came running with Mr. Owen not very far behind. And there was I halfway up the wall, when into the room above the kitchen went the thievin' scoundrel, and that was all, for Mr. Owen told me to stay where I was, although I was aching to have a go at him.'

'You didn't see him until he was at the window?' asked Folly.

'If I had, he wouldn't have got as far as the window,' Paddy assured him, grimly, 'and if I set eyes on him again he'll wish that he hadn't crept past Paddy O'Hara, and that's a fact. But I've no doubt of the way he came.'

He waited expectantly to be asked where it was, and Folly, taking his cue, was led out to a corner of the garden, overgrown with shrubs. In the garden next door a thick hedge ran right up to the wall. It was easy enough to climb unseen from there to the back of the Gantrys' house.

'That's probably how both of them came,' Folly said solemnly. 'We'll have this patch watched, Cunningham.'

Swelling with importance, Paddy heard Cunningham detailed to search the ground before it was too dark.

The Scotland Yard man returned with Jim and Angela to the house. Jim thought that Cunningham looked put out because he had been left behind. He wondered whether Folly had any ulterior motive, and learned that he had, as they approached the front door.

'Is Mr. Langford seriously ill, Mr. Gantry?'

'He's subject to these attacks, apparently,' Jim answered. 'They take it out of him, and he went to bed immediately after this one.'

'Before or after the burglary?'

'Before.'

'Did the burglar try to get in his room again?'

'He didn't have the chance to,' said Jim. 'The Langfords were there all the time.'

'I see. You're sure he searched nowhere else?'

'He couldn't have——'

'Oh but he could,' insisted Folly rather testily. Humouring Paddy was one thing, humouring Jim quite another. Besides, he was hungry. 'O'Hara certainly saw him at the window, but surely it has occurred to you that he might have been climbing *out*, his work finished? So dangerous, my dear fellow, to jump to unwarranted conclusions. In a twinkling they become, in your mind, established facts. Misleading, very.'

Jim said: 'You're right, of course. I didn't think of it.'

He felt humbled. Folly might *look* absurd, might even behave in an absurd way, but he was very far from being it. Angela and Marjorie had gone upstairs to Tub, and here was a wonderful opportunity to say what was in his mind. Should he—or shouldn't he? He looked doubtfully at his companion, so plump and pink; and then blurted out:

'I'm worried about Langford.'

Folly showed no surprise, no interest even; but his hands were still.

'Why?'

'I didn't like the symptoms of his seizure tonight,' said Jim. 'They usually followed a certain pattern, but this attack was very different from the one he had the first night he was here. His wife remarked on it.'

With a shock Jim met a shrewdness in Folly's glance that he had only sensed before. He was glad he had told him, but a little shiver of apprehension chilled his spine as he wondered what he had started.

'What's on your mind, Gantry?' The Yard man spoke gently.

'I wondered if it could be poisoning,' admitted Jim.

'Have you any reason for thinking so, apart from the different symptoms of this attack?'

Jim said slowly: 'Not a reason for thinking it *was* poison exactly, but one for being afraid that it might have been.'

'What is it?' asked Folly.

Jim was beginning to wish that he had not introduced the subject. Here was a man who would never let up. He chose his words carefully.

'Langford seems depressed at times—so depressed that it wouldn't really surprise me if he made an attempt to kill himself. His illness is incurable, he says, and he's very conscious of being a burden on his wife. I can only give you my impressions, I've nothing definite to go on, but when I saw him in that seizure, I wondered if he had poisoned himself. I'm not a bit sure that I ought to have told you this,' he added, the consequence of what he had said becoming more and more apparent to him. 'I don't want Mrs. Langford worried.'

'Naturally,' Folly murmured, 'most estimable. Such sentiments do you credit, and I will respect them. Can you describe the symptoms?'

Jim nodded.

'I may ask you to do so, to a medically professional ear, of course.'

Jim nodded again.

'Thank you,' said Folly. 'I will arrange for a good man to see you tonight or in the morning. You won't want the others to know about it, so you'd better let me give you a ring and make an appointment at the police station.'

'That's a good idea,' said Jim.

Folly smiled, and a suspicion of a strut showed in his gait.

'And let me assure you of this, Mr. Gantry. We shall work with utmost discretion and we shall not betray any confidence.' His voice, rich and full, rose a few tones as if to a mere afterthought. 'Unless, of course, in the interests of justice. If Langford were poisoned, for instance, there is the possibility —perhaps you had not thought of it?—that the poison was *not* self-administered.'

Jim looked at him steadily. 'Are you implying that Mrs. Langford——'

99

'Oh dear me no.' Folly's voice was now almost a squeak. 'Nothing like that. I'm simply pointing out the obvious facts.' He hesitated, as if trying to decide how far he should go, and then he added with a quick, apologetic smile, his eyes seeing, but appearing not to see, Jim's quickly changing expressions: 'I don't like prying into personal affairs, Gantry, but sometimes it is necessary. Have you any reason to believe that Mrs. Langford would like to get rid of her husband?'

Jim's violent denial was stilled. He remembered the incident on the staircase outside Andrew's temporary offices, and all that had followed it, but he also remembered the care with which Marjorie had looked after her husband that evening. On balance, he thought it would be safer to tell the whole truth. He looked about him, feeling disloyal, even treacherous, and yet inexpressibly glad to lay the burden down.

He said: 'No. There is talk about an attachment between Mrs. Langford and Andrew Dale. Knowing Andrew, I am quite sure that he would not conspire to—well, I may as well be blunt—conspire to murder. Nor do I believe Mrs. Langford capable of it. On the other hand, I know—I think—that they are fond of each other.'

There. It was out. He looked wretchedly at Folly who quickly, adroitly, brought relief. He said quietly: 'That is no news to me, but I'm particularly glad that you have been frank. If there's one thing which always leads to trouble, it's keeping things back. If we know that anyone is deliberately withholding evidence, we naturally wonder why, and can hardly be blamed if we then bark up the wrong tree.' Footsteps drew near. 'I'll telephone you about that appointment,' he promised hurriedly, and then turned to greet Cunningham and Owen.

They had nothing further to report. Cunningham ran through the description of the dark-haired man again, to make sure that the details were right, and then the police took themselves off.

Jim went upstairs. Angela was just coming out of the nursery. She closed the door softly.

'Have the police gone?' Jim nodded, 'Splendid! Have you seen Marjorie?'

'No, she's still in George's room.'

'I do wish I could help them,' Angela said. 'Anyway, I have an idea, darling.'

Jim said rather doubtfully: 'Have you?' For though Angela's ideas were sometimes brilliant, at others they could only be called disastrous. 'What is it?'

'One thing I *do* like is *enthusiasm*,' said Angela, making a face at him. 'I thought I might go to see Mrs. Dale.'

'Good heavens, no!'

'I knew you would oppose it,' said Angela sweetly, 'but I'm not a bit sure that you're right, Jim. She must have come to see Marjorie for some reason, and she must have wanted to see her pretty urgently, or she wouldn't have come by taxi and given us no warning. I thought if I went to the house and told her that Marjorie was very worried about George but also anxious to know what she—Mrs. Dale—wanted, I might learn something. I wouldn't go and ask her what she came for, of course; I'd just sit back and hope she'd give something away. She's one of those terribly clever women who can't imagine that anyone else has any brains. Don't you think it's a good idea?'

Jim's expression of obduracy began to break.

'Well, there *may* be something in it.'

'Then I'll go right away,' declared Angela, leaping up and kissing his cheek. 'Supper will have to be late but that won't matter much.'

'I wonder if I ought to come with you and wait outside,' said Jim, thoughtfully.

'No, this is *my* show,' Angela told him. 'You've had your huddle with that darling Folly, who gave me such an Edwardian compliment, and that reminds me that you haven't told me what you were talking about so earnestly yet. Have the story all ready for me by the time I come back, won't you?' She laughed, and Jim went to telephone for a taxi while she hurried upstairs.

When she had left, he decided that he had been a fool to let her go. If Mrs. Dale annoyed her Angela might, and probably would, forget all discretion. The visit would seem unnatural, and yet—Mrs. Dale was the type of woman who considered that her wishes were more or less commands, and who would expect people to consult her.

He hoped Angela would not be gone for long.

Angela was in high spirits when she reached the Dales'
house in Marlborough Avenue. It was only a few doors away
from old Coombs's house, and it stood well back from the road
in grounds of nearly an acre. There was a street lamp immediately outside it, but the house itself was in darkness. Angela
paid and dismissed the taxi-driver, and hurried up the steps.
The door was opened, after a wait of some minutes, by a
middle-aged woman, who ushered her into the hall.

It was the first time Angela had visited Andrew Dale's
house, and she did not think Jim had ever been there. That
was rather surprising, since Andrew and he were such good
friends. Angela had never thought of this before, but now she
put it down to a difficult mother. Miserable old battle-axe——

The maid reappeared.

'Mrs. Dale will see you,' she said, 'if you will please wait in
here.'

The room into which Angela was led was spacious and well-
furnished in an old-fashioned way. It was an attractive room.
Everything about it suggested wealth and good taste; and
Angela was agreeably surprised.

She was alone for nearly ten minutes, and was beginning to
feel impatient, when the door opened and Mrs. Dale swept
in.

Swept was the only word for it. She wore a dinner gown
which touched the floor, and she seemed to walk with a
deliberate stateliness.

'I understand that you wish to see me, Mrs. Gantry,' said
the older woman. She waved to a chair, sitting down herself on
a couch that would do full justice to her flowing skirts.

'You're very kind,' said Angela. A 'little girl' manner would
go down best with Mrs. Dale, she decided—sweet innocence
full of admiration for so great a personage. 'I want to see you,
Mrs. Dale, because my husband told me that you called to see
Marjorie——'

'You refer to Mrs. Langford?' inquired Andrew's mother.

'Yes,' agreed Angela, and put another mark against this
woman. She did not show her feelings, but went on pleasantly: 'I told her that you called and she was very sorry that

102

she couldn't come to see you tonight. George—her husband—was taken ill; I think my husband told you.' She waved her hand, vaguely. 'And Marjorie was so upset that I took it upon myself to come and see whether I could take back any message.'

'That was thoughtful of you,' said Mrs. Dale, with a queenly inclination of her head. 'I do not think that there is any message that I can send through a third party, Mrs. Gantry, and Mrs. Langford should have realised that——'

'Oh, I'm sure she did! Coming here was my idea, and I do realise that it was a little presumptuous, but I was troubled because you had had a wasted journey.'

'Then, in the circumstances you mention, Mrs. Langford is hardly to blame,' Mrs. Dale admitted. 'As for the purpose of my call, Mrs. Gantry, it is not one which I feel I can divulge but I will go so far as to tell you that I am *extremely* worried about my son, and I think it most unfortunate that Mrs. Langford is staying in Malling. She is aware . . .'

It all came out.

There was nothing very much in it, Angela decided, except that it confirmed her impression of Mrs. Dale. She had visited the house to tell Marjorie that in her opinion she should leave Malling because her presence had a disturbing effect on Andrew. As a married woman, she should have the decency to realise that. She had made her own bed, Mrs. Dale said with relish, and she must lie on it. Naturally, one felt sorry for a woman who was tied to a chronic invalid, but she had entered into this marriage with her eyes open.

There was a lot more, and Angela listened with exemplary patience. The interview lasted for half-an-hour, after which Mrs. Dale rose to her full height and graciously extended her hand.

'You've been so good,' murmured Angela, 'and I do understand. I feel rather guilty, Mrs. Dale, because Mar—Mrs. Langford is staying at my house. I had no idea of the real position.'

'In my opinion,' declared Mrs. Dale, 'you would be wise to put an end to her visit, Mrs. Gantry.'

Outside, Angela strode down the drive muttering to herself. The unprintable old cat! The shrew! The troublemaking, hypocritical old buzzard! She would tell Jim exactly what she thought of her. How on earth had Andrew come to have such a mother? All along Marlborough Avenue she stormed to herself. She could hear Mrs. Dale's voice in her ears, grating, condescending, scandal-mongering. How she had kept her patience she did not know. How such people *lived* she did not know. She had always been right not to make friends in Malling. The town must do something to its residents.

Between Marlborough Avenue and the main road, where she would be able to catch her bus, was another long, tree-lined road. There were houses and gateways about every forty yards, high walls on one side, beech trees on the other. Her furious frame of mind made her oblivious of everything about her. It was not until she turned a corner and reached a gateway where two shadows were thrown by the light from a window, that she noticed anything at all. The shadows moved away. She searched for them unavailingly. A nervous moment passed as she approached the gateway. She heard two people giggling. In relief, she realised that she had passed a courting couple.

The relief was short-lived. It was difficult to concentrate on Mrs. Dale's shortcomings now. She was aware of the poor lighting in this road. Car headlights in the main thoroughfare seemed a long way off. Very few of the houses had lighted windows at the front, and the place seemed filled with shadows.

There was a sound behind her.

Someone *was* following her! In alarm, she threw a glance over her shoulder, but could see no one. She quickened her pace. The other footsteps seemed to quicken, too. She did not look behind her again, but her heart was beating fast and she had completely forgotten Mrs. Dale. How she wished she had not sent the taxi away!

She told herself that she was a fool—she was just imagining things. There was no one behind her, why on earth should there be? But a few seconds later she heard the footsteps quite distinctly. They seemed nearer. The end of the road was still a long way off. If she ran, perhaps she would outdistance her pursuer, perhaps she would get to the main road safely. No, she mustn't run. It would prove that she was frightened.

A cyclist came out of a gateway immediately in front of her, light wobbling, tyres crunching on the gravel. She stifled a gasp, and then wished she had called out, but he was too far away now. She dared to look behind again. She could hear nothing. Had it been all her imagination?

Hands came out of the darkness and gripped her arms.

She screamed.

Another hand was clapped over her mouth, stifling the scream. She stiffened with terror—and then she felt as she had done when the dark-haired man had rushed out into the drive. She started to struggle. The grip on her arms grew tighter, then leapt to her throat.

She felt her bag snatched from her hand as a blow on the side of her head sent her reeling against the wall. Slowly she collapsed on to the pavement.

But she was alone!

Her throat was painful, she could hardly breathe, her heart was beating at a tremendous rate, but she was in no further danger; the men had gone. As she realised that, she began to cry.

A car turned out of a gateway, the headlights glaring towards her. She heard the driver put on the brakes. A man jumped out of the car, followed by a woman, and they ran towards her.

'I—I'm all right,' she muttered, knowing herself to be babbling like a fool, 'I'm all right, really.'

A faint whiff of perfume came from the woman as she bent over Angela. The man's arms, strong and gentle, lifted her to her feet.

'Are you sure you're all right?'

'Yes, perfectly, thank you,' gasped Angela. 'I was so frightened. The men——' She paused.

'What men?' asked the woman.

'They—they sprang out on me from a gateway,' Angela said wildly. 'One of them held my throat, the other took my handbag.'

She sensed a certain scepticism as the woman took a torch from her pocket and shone it about. There was no sign of Angela's bag.

Angela took a deep breath, and tried to speak calmly.

'I wonder if you would take me to the police station? My name is Mrs. Gantry, and——'

'Mrs. *Gantry*!' exclaimed the man, as if that explained the whole mystery. 'It's Mrs. Gantry,' he repeated to the woman, with the air of a man who had made a great discovery. 'You know, the O'Hara fellow——' He turned back to Angela. 'Of course we'll take you to the police station,' he said warmly. 'We were going into Malling to have dinner with some friends. I wish—hallo, who's this?'

A man had appeared out of the darkness. They had not heard him until that moment. He must have been standing just outside the glow of light. He was short and plump and smiling. A hat was tilted to the back of his head, and they could see the gleam of his teeth.

'Who are you?' demanded Angela's rescuer.

'Oh, I'm quite harmless,' said the stranger. 'My name's Lecky. I know Mrs. Gantry. That is, I brought her some good news this morning. Do you remember me, Mrs. Gantry?'

Angela looked at him vaguely.

'We're taking Mrs. Gantry in to the police station,' said the man, brusquely. 'Open the door, Jane, will you?'

'Oh, let me,' offered Lecky.

He not only opened the door, he begged a lift into the town. On the way, he got the whole story out of Angela, and as she went into the police station with her two companions, she saw him go into a telephone kiosk. It was as she entered the hall that she wondered how he had come to be in the shadows, and whether he knew anything about the assault on her.

CHAPTER TWELVE

MEDICAL OPINION

When Jim heard Folly's voice, he thought it was about the appointment with the doctor. Then Folly said 'She's quite all right now,' and he pricked up his ears. 'Will you come out to fetch her?' Folly added.

Jim's heart missed a beat: '*Fetch* her? Fetch *whom*?'

'Your wife had an accident,' Folly began, and then there was an explosive comment from someone standing near the telephone, and a voice which sounded like Angela's, saying: 'It wasn't an accident! Let me speak to him.'

Twenty minutes later, Jim was on the way to the police station driven by one of Cunningham's men. He had told only Paddy where he was going. Marjorie was upstairs with George, and he did not want to alarm her. He was on tenterhooks as the car sped along the main road, and jumped out immediately it pulled up outside the police station.

A policeman said: 'Upstairs, first door on the right, sir.'

Not until he saw Angela sitting in an easy-chair, with a cup of tea by her side, did he believe that she was really all right.

Folly and Cunningham were with her.

'Oh, darling!' Jim took her in his arms, and for a moment quite forgot that there were others present. Then he put her gently aside and turned angrily to the two policemen.

'You people are making a pretty fine mess of it, aren't you?'

'Oh, Jim——' began Angela.

'Leave this to me,' said Jim, savagely. 'You've wasted your time watching the house. You've followed me every time I've left it, and you've also followed my wife—until tonight, when it could have been of some help. What the devil's the matter with you all?'

At his tone Cunningham had stiffened at once, but Folly

remained calm and imperturbable. He spread his hands.

'You're right, of course, Mr. Gantry. The house is still watched, and Mrs. Gantry should have been followed. I am already making inquiries about the man who replaced Detective-Sergeant Owen.'

'It's time you stopped making inquiries and got something done,' growled Jim. 'I would not have let her go on her own had I not felt that you people would look after her. In future, I suggest you either leave us alone, or make quite sure that capable men are watching the house.'

'We'll do everything we can,' Folly assured him. 'I think the explanation of what went wrong tonight is simple, Mr. Gantry. The man on duty had no car, and Mrs. Gantry left suddenly, by taxi.'

'It's no use worrying about what's happened,' Jim said, 'it's what is going to happen that worries me. Have you any idea why my wife was attacked?'

Cunningham said: 'I thought you said——' and then he broke off abruptly, but Jim caught the drift of his meaning, and looked at him with some annoyance.

'Yes, I did say that I was worried about what is going to happen, not what has happened. I'm trying to make sure that a similar thing can't happen again. If we know why she was attacked, that ought to help.'

'And it will,' said Folly. 'Obviously, robbery was the motive.'

'That's what I can't understand,' broke in Angela. 'There was practically nothing in my bag. I had enough to pay the taxi-driver and a few shillings over, a lipstick and a compact, a handkerchief and—oh yes—a snapshot of Tub. Hardly worth an assault.'

Folly said: 'Well, I suppose it could have been a shot in the dark. Sometimes lady's handbags are fruitful prizes for pickpockets.' He paused a moment, and then went on with a casualness that deceived Angela but caused Jim to prick up his ears: 'You didn't bring anything away from Mrs. Dale's, did you?'

Angela shook her head.

If Folly was disappointed he hid it well. Geniality enveloped him, and just that touch of buffoonery that Cunningham found both fascinating and unsettling. He almost danced to the door, emitting a series of squeaks designed to convey sympathy, reassurance and valediction.

The interview was over.

Angela and Jim said little on the way home; it was after the car had driven off and they were walking arm-in-arm along the drive that Angela referred to the police.

'Darling, weren't you just a *little* sharp with Folly?'

Jim laughed shortly. 'I wasn't half as sharp as I felt like being. Bunglers!'

'I think it's Cunningham's fault,' said Angela. 'He was standing there and glowering all the time. I think he's sore because Scotland Yard have been brought in.'

'Cunningham's all right really,' Jim assured her. 'The truth is that the Malling police aren't accustomed to cases like this; it's outside their routine. Folly has to do the best he can with men who work at a much slower pace than he's accustomed to.'

They reached the front door, and went in. There was a glow of light from the doorway leading to the kitchen, but all the rest of the house was in darkness.

Paddy came hurrying to meet them.

'Good evening to ye,' he greeted, with his usual smile. 'Is it tea or cocoa you'll be having, Mrs. Gantry, or will ye have a strong drink for once in a while?'

'I want something to eat, not drink,' Angela said.

'Sure and ye do. I've a pie hotting in the oven; it will melt in your mouth, so it will. Will ye be telling the others that supper's ready, or shall I tell them myself?'

'I'll tell them,' said Angela.

Rather wearily she climbed the stairs and tapped softly on Marjorie's door, which opened almost at once.

'He's asleep,' Marjorie whispered.

'Then creep out without disturbing him,' murmured Angela. 'Supper'll be ready in ten minutes.'

Angela and Jim went on to their own room, and as they entered, Angela turned suddenly and flung her arms about her husband. She clung so tightly that Jim, alarmed, realised as he had not done before just how terrified she had been.

'I was frightened *stiff*!' she declared.

'So would I have been,' said Jim. 'You came out of it very

well, my darling. I suppose the police asked you whether you recognised either of the beggars.'

'Yes, and I didn't. Oh, Jim, I do love you!'

'And as I told you when Cunningham was standing at the door at the very start of this affair, I love *you*,' declared Jim, trying to steer Angela's highly emotional state back to normal. He kissed the tip of her nose. 'You'd better get your things off. We don't want Marjorie to be waiting for us alone, and Paddy will go up in the air if we let his precious pie get cold.'

He watched as Angela ran a comb through her hair. Her movements were graceful, and he loved the way she tilted her head towards the glass. The house was very quiet. It was hard to believe that only an hour or so before, someone had leapt upon her out of the darkness.

'Why on earth should it have happened to *me*,' mused Angela.

Jim said shortly, wondering whether it was best to let her talk about it or not to let her talk about it: 'Someone was watching Mrs. Dale's house, and thought you had brought something away with you. They wanted that something.'

Angela stared at him. 'Are you serious?'

'Of course I'm serious.'

'The police didn't hint at anything like that.'

'The police think they are being clever,' said Jim. 'Oh, it's nothing to worry about. Your assailants know now that you hadn't got it—I mean whatever they were looking for—and that's that. But it's a queer business. Had the police asked you before whether you had brought anything from Mrs. Dale?'

'Yes,' said Angela, 'that was one of the first questions they asked me. I don't know what I would have done if those two people hadn't come along. They were a charming couple, darling, named Allison. We'll have to meet them—I ought to go tomorrow and thank them for all they did.' Her thoughts had strayed from the assault, now, to Jim's relief. He had been afraid that she might brood over it. 'There aren't many pleasant couples in Malling, as far as I can see. There are far too many dragons like Mrs. Dale. Ugh!'

Jim would have preferred not to let Marjorie know what had happened, but Angela could not keep it to herself. Marjorie was at first startled to hear of the visit to Mrs. Dale, then, apparently, amused. Angela got into her stride over the story of the assault, giving Jim a chance to collect his thoughts.

They were not reassuring.

He was sure that the assailants had expected to find something in Angela's bag. It was just possible that they had hoped to find the will, although he had nothing but guesswork to go on. He fancied that the police would guess along the same lines, and was not at all sure that they were satisfied with the reason Angela had given for her excursion. Knowing just how Angela's mind worked, he knew that she had acted on impulse, but the police probably thought that she had a very different purpose in view.

There were other aspects of the incident. Lecky's part, for instance. Had he turned up just by accident? Had he followed Angela to the Dales' house? Was it possible that he had taken part in the assault? The police would certainly be alive to that possibility. Lecky had become almost a sinister figure of mystery to Jim; the man's attitude had always been difficult to understand, but of his ability there was no doubt. Perhaps he had an ulterior motive, one which was conveniently hidden by his ostensible occupation. Lecky was worth attention.

And what of the immediate future?

If two men had attacked Angela because they thought she had brought something from Mrs. Dale, would they be satisfied, now that they had searched her handbag and found nothing of interest? They might think that Angela had put the mysterious 'something' into her pocket. They might have another shot at getting it. They had been persistent enough in trying to search the Langfords' luggage, and had also proved their resourcefulness.

Why had Mrs. Dale come to see Marjorie?

Angela was convinced that she now knew the reason but Jim was by no means certain. Mrs. Dale would hardly have gone to such trouble to tell Marjorie to leave someone else's house. Had she wanted to drive Marjorie away, she would surely have launched her attack on him or Angela. More likely, she had wanted a private talk with Marjorie. When Angela had turned up, she had put out the smoke screen of scandalous gossip. In other words, Mrs. Dale wasn't quite the fool that Angela assumed.

111

He wondered if Andrew knew about the visit.

The telephone bell rang.

'All right, I'll go,' he said, and went out into the hall.

He lifted the receiver.

'I'm sorry to worry you again so soon, Mr. Gantry,' came Folly's voice; soft, almost purring in quality. 'I wonder if you could have that chat with the doctor if I send a car out for you at once?'

'Yes,' said Jim, 'provided I can be sure my house is well watched in my absence.'

'You have my word for it.'

'Thanks. I'll be ready.'

Neither Marjorie nor Angela liked the idea of him going out again, and Angela seemed nervous. Jim reassured her as best he could and Paddy, who was clearing away the supper things, declared that he would bring a chair into the hall and sit there near the sitting-room door until Jim returned.

Three policemen stood in the porch when Jim opened the door in answer to a ring. A car was standing in the drive. One of the policemen was Owen.

'The Inspector thought you might like me to stay inside the house until you're back, sir,' he said, a trifle sheepishly.

'Sure and it's a waste of time,' declared Paddy, from the dining-room door. 'Paddy O'Hara will be on duty and no one will get past *him*.'

'It's just as you like, sir,' Owen said to Jim.

'Do ye play draughts?' demanded Paddy unexpectedly.

'A little,' Owen said, in surprise.

'Och, then ye can stay and I'll wipe the floor wid ye,' declared Paddy.

Jim was still smiling as he was driven along the main road. It was surprising how he had accepted the disruption of their quiet way of life. If George had not been taken ill, he would almost have enjoyed it. The more he thought of Marjorie's husband, the more he liked him. It was hateful to feel that an attempt might have been made to poison him and that Marjorie *might* be the poisoner. The thought was repugnant, and yet he had to face it: undoubtedly the police had it in mind.

They did not go to the police station, but went on to a house just off the High Street. Here Dr. Lawson lived. Jim knew that he was the police surgeon as well as a general practitioner, and the most popular doctor in the town.

He had not previously met him, and expected to find an elderly man. Instead, he found a man of no more than fifty, tall, well-groomed, with attractive iron-grey hair.

They shook hands.

'Sit down, Mr. Gantry. The police have given me some idea of what this is about,' said Lawson. 'It's a little odd to be asked to give a diagnosis without seeing the patient, of course, but it's probably worth trying. The police appear to think so, anyhow.'

Jim smiled. 'Yes. Well, what do you want to know?'

'Were you with the patient from the beginning of the attack?'

'No. I don't know for certain how long he had been ill. I gathered about ten minutes. He was shaking—trembling—and every now and again he writhed as if he were in great pain. Then he settled down and broke out into a cold sweat. His face had a greyish pallor—not blue, like it was the other night.'

'How long did this particular paroxysm last?'

'Well, he was getting better ten minutes or so after I arrived.'

'About twenty minutes in all, then?' suggested Lawson.

'Something like that.'

'And how was he afterwards?'

'Washed out,' said Jim. 'His colour became normal, but he hadn't any strength at all. He was sleeping an hour ago, and his wife told me that he seemed to be much better. Can you make anything of it?'

'There are several possible explanations,' said Lawson, evasively. 'Had he just eaten a meal?'

'It was about an hour after tea, I suppose.'

'Can you be more precise about that?'

'I might, on reflection,' said Jim, 'but so much has happened this evening that I'm a little vague at the moment. I'll try to work it out, if you like.'

'Try now,' said Lawson.

Jim frowned in concentration. So much had happened. But he mustn't muddle things up. This was important. He pulled himself together. The afternoon had been quiet enough after

113

the excitement of Paddy's return. The next real excitement had not come until the attempt to break into the house. Tub had been out at a party. They had had tea at a quarter-past four. Then Andrew had arrived, followed by the police. It was after the police and Andrew had gone that George had the attack.

Rather confusedly, and with at least two corrections, Jim painstakingly went over it.

'Splendid,' said Lawson. 'That will help a lot. Did Mr. Langford eat anything between meals?'

'I don't think so.'

'Did he take medicine regularly, do you know?'

'I heard some talk of powders, but I never saw him take one,' said Jim. 'He's a chronic invalid, I rather gather that he's been given up as incurable. I'm afraid I don't know what the trouble is, except that it's the aftermath of exposure—he had a rough time in the early part of the war.'

'I see,' said Lawson. 'Do you know the name of his London doctor?'

'I'm afraid not.'

'Hmm.' Lawson leaned back in his chair. 'Can you think of anything else that might be helpful?'

He listened intently as Jim went over the first attack, making notes all the time.

When he had first arrived, Jim had felt that there was little point in this interview. Now he was not so sure. Lawson had created a good impression; he was a man who would be on top of his job, and would miss little. Folly was no fool, either; he had deliberately omitted to ask Jim to get information from George or Marjorie; the probable reason was his anxiety to make sure that the Langfords did not know that the inquiry was being made. Provided neither of them had anything to do with it, it was as well for their peace of mind that they did not know the police suspected poisoning.

The telephone bell rang. Lawson turned to pick up the receiver, and Jim looked away from him. For the first time he noticed a second door, standing ajar. A light was on in the room beyond. It puzzled him, until he saw a shadow against the wall. A man was sitting at a table, and Jim could even see the shadow of a pencil which he held in his hand.

He felt a sudden surge of anger. *The police were in there, taking everything down in shorthand.*

'I think that's all,' said Jim, rising, 'and I must get back; my wife is rather jumpy.'

Before Lawson could stop him, he made for the wrong door. The shadow moved.

'No, that's not the door,' Lawson said, hastily, but by then Jim had pushed it wide open and saw Folly.

CHAPTER THIRTEEN

ALARM!

Too angry to be reasonable, Jim strode into the street. The police car was waiting.

'Ready, sir?' asked the driver.

'You'll need that for Superintendent Folly,' Jim snapped, and went off towards the High Street, determined not to be beholden in any way to the police.

Before he had gone twenty yards he had cooled down a little, and even acknowledged that his reaction might be liable to be misunderstood. A few moments' reflection reassured him, however; he had acted naturally enough. There was no reason why the police should not have been present at the interview and taken the notes with his full knowledge. He had volunteered to help them, and should have been taken into their confidence. They could do their own work in future.

By now the buses had stopped running, and he would probably have some difficulty in getting a taxi. Well, it would do him no harm to walk, and he would be home in three-quarters of an hour.

He was in very much the same circumstances as Angela, when she had been attacked, but this road was well lit and there was no fear of being followed in darkness.

But there *was* someone close behind him.

He turned abruptly, expecting to see Folly.

Lecky smiled back at him. 'Want a lift, Gantry?'

'What the devil are you doing here?'

'Snooping,' replied Lecky. 'It's my job. It makes me unpopular, I know, but what's a cold shoulder now and again?' There was something about the man's geniality which eased Jim's annoyance. 'My car's just round the corner,' Lecky went on. 'We'll have you home in no time. Annoyed with the police?'

'Yes.'

'Dare a poor newspaperman ask why?'

'You've learned quite enough for one night,' said Jim grimly.

'I never learn enough,' declared Lecky. 'The more I know, the more helpful I can be.'

'You weren't very helpful when my wife was attacked,' Jim retorted, as they turned a corner where Lecky's small car was standing. 'I suppose as a newspaperman, you would have stood by and watched her being murdered, so that you could send a good story to your paper.'

'Now, now,' chided Lecky. 'I was speeding along the pavement to lend a hand when the car drew up. I wish it hadn't. I would have approached with stealth, and probably got a good look at the assailants' faces.'

'That's a fine story,' said Jim, only slightly mollified.

'That's because it's a true one.'

'How did you come to know that my wife was at Mrs. Dale's?'

Lecky let in the clutch and they moved off. He laughed.

'My, my, you're nearly as bad as the police. Folly and Cunningham questioned me for half an hour, and Cunningham still doesn't believe that I'm just after news. The answer is that I *didn't* know that your wife was at Mrs. Dale's house. I had intended to call on Mrs. Dale for an interview. I knew that if I went when Andrew Dale was there, he would quickly show me the door.'

'Naturally. He's got more than enough to worry about, without being pestered by reporters,' growled Jim.

'Oh, granted. I don't blame him, just wish that he would take a different attitude. I watched the house, hoping he would leave, and he did. He hadn't been gone five minutes before your wife arrived, so I waited until she had gone. And then I saw a man lurking in the shadows. He followed her. I followed him. It's simple, you see.'

'You seem to have plenty of luck,' said Jim.

'Not luck,' Lecky reproached him. 'In the best circles they call it a "nose for news". When I saw Folly go out tonight— you can't mistake the twinkle from those patent leather shoes —I thought he might be worth following up. He led me to Dr.

Lawson. When you arrived, I sat back contentedly,' added Lecky with a grin. 'I knew that you would take a sensible view and tell me what had transpired.'

'Then you're in for a disappointment,' declared Jim.

'Now, now. Tell your Uncle Lecky. Strictly off the record.'

'I'm not so sure about you keeping anything off the record,' Jim told him.

Lecky grew serious. 'My word on it, old chap.'

Rather pleased to give vent to his anger before it cooled, Jim recounted what had happened. It did not sound as heinous as he had hoped, and he began to wonder whether he had behaved foolishly after all.

When it was told, Lecky was laughing.

'That must have given Folly a jolt,' he said. 'On the other hand it might be exactly what the cunning old fox wanted.'

'What reason could he possibly have for behaving like that?'

Lecky glanced at him thoughtfully.

'My dear fellow, a very good one! To unnerve you. Folly's favourite method. Gets his suspects one by one and works on their nerves. Look how he's running this case. Two or three visits to you. A pleasant, friendly attitude most of the time, getting a little sharp now and again. Pretending that he's fully in sympahy with you, persuading you to take him into your confidence, and then doing something which makes you angry. It's deliberate, you know. He thinks he will make you jumpy that way; if you *have* got anything to hide, then you'll reveal it sooner or later. Don't underrate our Folly.'

Jim said slowly: 'How can he reasonably suspect me of having anything to do with this business?'

Lecky said: 'You're not at your best, are you?'

'I don't understand you,' declared Jim.

Lecky whistled. 'Don't you, by Jove! I suppose it's a case of not seeing the wood for the trees. The moment I give it a name, you'll understand why he's so interested.'

'Confound it, Paddy's practically cleared; he must know by now that I haven't handled stolen goods. I can't see what you're driving at.'

They pulled up outside the house, and Lecky put on the hand-brake thoughtfully.

'Can't you? Well, who had a motive for killing old Coombs?'

'You've already made that clear. The Langfords, and to a lesser degree, Andrew Dale. But——'

'And still you don't see,' marvelled Lecky. 'I'm disappointed in you, Gantry! Doesn't it strike you that if you were outside this business, instead of being so deeply involved, *you* would think it odd if someone opened their doors to a couple who were obviously the chief suspects in a murder case?'

Jim stared at him with the dawning of understanding.

'I thought you'd get it,' murmured Lecky. 'Now, what have you told the police? The same as you've told me: that the Langfords were sprung on you; you hardly knew them before, but you threw open wide the doors of Welcome Hall and have gone to considerable trouble to help them. The police are cynical people, you know. They know the world. There *are* generous and kind-hearted folk who will do that kind of thing, but they're few and far between. Folly thinks that you allowed the Langfords to come because you're involved, and for no other reason.'

'The damned fool!' exploded Jim.

'Who? You or he?' demanded Lecky with a chuckle. 'Believe me, I would reason on the same lines. And look at the evidence to support such suspicions. Paddy *might* have been the thief at Coombs's house. He can't be ruled out entirely. He might have been working for you. He's almost one of the family, as you've told me yourself, and you allow him a fair amount of licence, don't you? Not many people would let a servant talk as you let Paddy talk.'

'You simply don't know Paddy,' said Jim.

'Possibly, possibly,' Lecky said airily. 'I'm simply trying to show you how the police mind works—and Folly *is* a policeman, and a mighty shrewd one at that. Don't kid yourself that anyone so fond of food and handmade shoes is automatically brainless! Paddy, then, *might* have killed Coombs, and *you* might have conspired with the Langfords, your reward being a cut in their inheritance when it comes.'

'Of all the crazy nonsense——'

Lecky shrugged, then put a hand on Jim's arm.

'It's logical enough. But even if it were not, there are other

119

things to justify Folly keeping an eye on you.'

'Such as?'

'The two burglars who got away,' said Lecky. 'Both the man who searched the Langfords' luggage and the man this afternoon got into your house without any trouble, although the police were watching. Has Folly pointed out to you the fact that the man this afternoon might have been spotted coming *out*, rather than going *in*?'

Jim nodded.

'Characteristic of Folly! Supposing you knew that the man had been inside the house all the time? Supposing you were involved in this business, and were deliberately attempting to hoodwink the police? What would be better than to *pretend* to have a burglary, catch the police at a disadvantage, blame them for allowing the man to get away, and all the time be laughing up your sleeve? It's a possibility, isn't it?'

'Why should I stage a burglary?' demanded Jim, but he already saw, with a sinking heart, what Lecky was driving at.

'That's simple,' Lecky answered. 'You want to establish the fact that there is *another* burglar, that O'Hara can't possibly be the man concerned. Therefore, you put on an act, prove the existence of another burglar, put O'Hara up to telling the story about the man in the market-place from whom he made his many purchases, and cleverly point a finger away from you and your household. Very neat, isn't it?'

Jim said: 'Can Folly be thinking like that?'

'Believe me, he can, and probably is,' declared Lecky. 'Oh, I don't mean that he assumes you're guilty, but he's allowing for the possibility. That explains his little trick at the surgery. If you think you're getting away with something, what could be better than a jolt like that? It would unnerve you. It did make you angry. You see,' went on Lecky, gently, 'if Folly had wanted to take notes of that talk with Lawson, nothing would have been easier than to make sure you didn't find out. I don't think for one moment that he was taking notes. He staged it so that you should *think* he was. He *meant* you to spot him.'

Jim drew in a deep breath.

'After my flare-up, he'll probably feel that he's right,' he said. 'I was a bigger fool than I realised.'

'Well, you could have been at that,' said Lecky candidly.

'I'm only telling you.'

'Well, now you've told me,' Jim said a trifle coldly. 'I take it that's the lot?'

'My dear chap, there's the most curious thing of all,' said Lecky, cheerfully, his spirits seeming to rise as Gantry's fell. 'Why did your wife go to visit Mrs. Dale? No, no, I'm not asking you; I'm putting the question in Folly's mouth. He can't answer it. He must think it odd, especially since he knows that Mrs. Dale called here. Now, you've told him that she called to see Marjorie. There isn't any proof of that. There isn't any proof that you and your wife didn't talk to her, and that the visit to the Dales' house wasn't prearranged. To further the mystery, your wife was attacked as she came away. *Why?* Because someone had reason to believe that she would come away with something valuable in her possession. The only thing missing in this affair, as far as we yet know, is old Coombs's will. It's at least possible that the will disinherits the Langfords. If your wife was ever an agent of the Langfords, she might have gone to collect the will from Mrs. Dale.'

Jim said desperately: 'But how would you explain *her* collusion?'

'I don't think anyone can explain that yet,' said Lecky, 'but they can look for evidence that there is collusion between you, the Langfords, and Mrs. Dale. There's some evidence of it. Ostensibly, the Langfords came here because Mrs. Dale wouldn't let them stay in her house. Rather arbitrary, don't you think, especially with Langford so ill? It could easily have been stage-managed to make it look as if the Langfords and Mrs. Dale are at loggerheads. Why did she call on Mrs. Langford today, or on you? Surely the reasonable thing would be for her to keep away. Your wife's explanation of what she said isn't exactly convincing. *Would* any woman talk quite so freely about another as Mrs. Dale did about Mrs. Langford? Yes, yes, I know some *might*,' went on Lecky, 'but on such a short acquaintance, it isn't likely. Folly would be perfectly justified in thinking that your wife pitched a cock-and-bull story.'

'She needn't have asked to be taken to the police station,' Jim objected.

Lecky chuckled. 'The trouble with you, Gantry, is that you're unpractised in the ways of trickery and deceit. Suppos-

121

ing your wife *was* involved in this business? She would know that the couple who rescued her would tell the police, so she would have to see them sooner or later. She would have the wit to realise that if she volunteered to see them, her innocence would look more convincing. Oh, Folly would have an answer to everything; don't make any mistake about that.'

They sat in silence. The street was dark, but a light was coming from Angela's room; Jim could see her moving about. Somewhere near by the police were watching, and Owen and Paddy were keeping their vigil inside the house. All of these things passed fleetingly through Jim's mind; he could not get over Lecky's analysis of the situation.

'I hope this isn't too much of a blow,' said Lecky. 'I quite thought you would be on to it.'

'It's pretty startling,' Jim said. 'But I'm very glad I know. Have you told anyone else about this?'

'Certainly not,' Lecky assured him, 'and believe me, I am on your side. I liked you when I first saw you,' he explained. Though these words were not particularly convincing, Jim let them pass. 'What we've got to do is to find the murderer,' Lecky added.

Jim said: 'But Cunningham told me they've discovered that the red-haired man, whom Paddy bought the stuff from, does exist, though they haven't got him yet.'

'Well, yes—Folly's method again. First disarm you, then give you a jolt.'

'I see,' said Jim, and he laughed shortly. 'Well, it's given me plenty to think about. You're very outspoken, Lecky. You haven't anything else up your sleeve, I hope.'

'Not even a rabbit,' Lecky assured him. 'Now, off you go. Er—shall you tell your wife?'

'Not yet,' said Jim.

'Wise man,' approved Lecky, and patted his arm as he got out of the car. 'I'll be seeing you.'

The car moved off. Jim walked up the drive, plunged in thought. If at first he had been inclined to scoff at the situation as Lecky saw it, he certainly was not now. It was too serious and complicated for that. He saw, as Lecky had seen, that a complete case could be built against him and the Langfords. If only Andrew had never suggested them coming here!

Was George a victim of poisoning?

He went upstairs. Paddy and Owen were on the landing, with a draught-board between them, and Paddy's broad grin told a tale of success. Owen got up.

'I should get to bed now, Paddy,' Jim said. 'You're not thinking of staying the night, Owen, are you?'

'If you'd like me to, I will,' said Owen, promptly.

Jim said casually: 'As to that, you must please yourself.' If he insisted on Owen leaving, it might look as if he had something to hide.

He went on into the bedroom, feeling in such a tangle of intrigue that he wondered if he would ever get free again.

He expected Angela to be wide awake and full of questions. His mind was in such a whirl that he doubted whether he could answer them. Angela, however, looked at him sleepily.

'Has anything happened?'

'No, I had a quiet journey,' said Jim. 'There's nothing fresh.'

'That's good.'

She was asleep when Jim got into bed. He lay awake for a long time, staring into the darkness, Lecky's story running through his mind. The logic was quite convincing: no wonder Folly suspected that he was involved.

There was a heavy post next morning. Several editors wanted reviews of new books quickly, and it was impossible for Jim to set all the work aside. George was so much better that he was able to get up for breakfast. He assured Jim that he would be happy enough downstairs with a book. Angela and Marjorie planned to go shopping. The two girls left a little after ten o'clock, taking Tub and the little push-cart. Jim watched them go, then turned and tried to get down to work.

One thing was helpful. Angela seemed to be completely undisturbed. She had been at her brightest that morning, and Tub on his best behaviour. Marjorie, too, seemed light-hearted, perhaps because of George's quick recovery.

Shopping done, tired but contented after a cup of coffee at one of the big stores, Angela suggested that they might as well get back. Marjorie, however, had been less successful in finding the exact shade of stockings that she wanted.

'There's a little shop along here where we might be lucky,' she said, 'it won't take a minute.'

The shop was in a side street, near the main road. Tub was left outside in his cart. Inside the shop, Angela and Marjorie concentrated on the various tints of beige and grey. A new quota had come in that morning, and they lost themselves in the absorbing task.

'Well,' said Angela, as they waited for their change, 'I haven't known a morning's shopping go as smoothly as this for years. *Three* pairs! And Tub will look sweet in that pale blue suit; I'm dying to see him in it.' She beamed at the shop assistant. 'Thank you so much,' she said, and led the way outside.

Tub wasn't there.

CHAPTER FOURTEEN

DESPAIR

Angela stood quite still, a savage terror striking at her heart.

She looked up and down the street, but there was no sign of Tub.

Not far off she glimpsed a policeman, and she walked towards him. There were dozens of prams, dozens of children sitting in them, and walking beside them.

She reached the policeman, and stood in front of him. He looked at her curiously. Then she spoke, her voice flat and expressionless.

'Officer, my baby has disappeared from outside Lang's shop.'

'I beg your pardon, ma'am?'

Tensely, Angela said: 'I mean it. I left him in his cart while I went inside. I was there for about ten minutes. Both he and the cart have vanished.'

'Vanished?' echoed the policeman. 'Have you looked for him, ma'am? He might have got out of the cart, and——'

'He wouldn't have taken it with him,' Angela said. 'I want you to report his disappearance at once.'

'He might have toddled off——' began the policeman.

Angela shouted: 'Don't stand there wasting time! The child's vanished, I tell you!' Her voice rose, and people stopped to stare at her. The policeman said soothingly:

'Now don't you worry, ma'am; he'll turn up. Like as not they'll have him at the police station if he wandered off. It's surprising what these toddlers can do, you know.' He rested a friendly hand on Angela's arm. 'He'll be all right.'

'*Are you going to report it at once?*'

'Why, yes, ma'am. If you'll come with me——'

'I want to stand here and watch for him,' Angela said. 'Tell

125

Sergeant Cunningham. No! Tell Superintendent Folly. I am Mrs. Gantry.'

'Mrs. Gantry!' exclaimed the policeman, thoughtfully. 'You—you'll stay about here, ma'am, won't you?'

'Yes,' said Angela, tensely.

By now a small crowd had gathered about her. Two or three women started to speak at once.

Angela hardly noticed them. She saw Tub in her mind's eye. Tub, pink-faced and blue-eyed, with his quick, beaming smile. Tub, doing exactly what he was told that morning, and being made much of by the shop assistants. *Tub!*

She stared at every child who passed, tried to look on the other side of the road and in both directions at once. No one had the courage to speak to her. Her face was chalk white, her eyes feverishly bright.

A woman came forward and touched her arm.

'I shouldn't worry, dear,' she said. 'I expect the policeman was right; it is surprising what they get up to. I should know, I've had *six*.'

Angela smiled mechanically.

'You're very kind.'

A well-dressed woman reached the crowd, and looked at Angela. A glance of recognition followed: she was Mrs. Allison, her rescuer the previous night.

She forced her way through the crowd.

'Hallo, Mrs. Gantry. Is it true?'

Angela said: 'He was outside Lang's, and missing when I left the shop. He's never got out of his straps before. The cart was gone, too.'

Mrs. Allison had the sense not to try to be reassuring.

'Have you told your husband?'

'No, no, I——'

'Can I telephone him for you?'

'Would you?'

'Yes, of course. What is your number?'

'Malling 331.'

Mrs. Allison hurried off, and Angela maintained her constant, useless vigil. By now the crowd had thinned out. Those who had thought she was making too much of it, began to influence her. Perhaps she was. Tub was surprisingly agile,

126

and very good at undoing straps and buckles. He also loved to push anything on wheels. The policeman was probably right; there was really no need to worry.

Of course there was need to worry!

Mrs. Allison came back.

'I've told him that you'll be at this corner or else in the police station,' she said.

'Thank you so much,' said Angela, and forced a smile. 'I keep trying to tell myself that there's nothing to worry about.'

'You'll be laughing about it when he comes back,' said Mrs. Allison. She was a good-looking brunette, smart and attractive. 'I lost my younger daughter once, she was missing for nearly two hours, but she came back safe and sound. It often happens, you know. Have you any other children?'

'No, only Tub.'

'I've two girls and a boy,' said Mrs. Allison. 'The boy is only six months.'

She talked quietly and sensibly. The street was thronged, though no one, now, did more than glance curiously at her as they passed. It was soothing to hear Mrs. Allison's voice, to be told about her children. Two were at a boarding school not far from Malling. She did not look old enough to have girls of eleven and nine—she could hardly be more than thirty.

A man came teetering along the street. Considering his bulk and the extreme smallness of his feet it was surprising how much ground he covered in so short a time. A pure silk scarf was knotted about his neck. It was, of course, Superintendent Folly.

He came to a halt beside Angela.

'I'm very sorry about this, Mrs. Gantry.'

'Have you *done* anything?' asked Angela. She hardly recognised her own voice.

'Yes,' said Folly. 'A full description of your son has been given to all our men on duty and a general call has been put out. I thought it better not to take any chances, although I think it likely that he'll turn up very soon, you know.'

'Yes,' said Angela.

If only she could think more clearly. The police had a description of Tub, a general call had been put out, *Folly was afraid that he had been kidnapped*. That was the only possible

127

explanation of the steps he had taken. Tub, kidnapped; perhaps by murderers. She swayed.

Folly went on: 'Mr. Lecky saw you a little while ago and was able to tell me what clothes your son was wearing, and Sergeant Cunningham knows the boy well, of course. I really don't think you have any cause for anxiety.'

'Thank you,' said Angela, stiffly.

Folly said: 'If you will allow me I will send for a car, to take you home. I'll see that you are telephoned immediately I have news.'

As he spoke, a taxi drew up and Jim jumped out.

'Oh, Jim!' she exclaimed, and tears flooded her eyes. 'Oh, Jim!'

He gripped her hands. 'Now steady,' he said, 'the young scamp's run out on us, that's all.'

'No, I don't believe he could,' she said. 'I don't believe he would have gone far, even if he'd got out of the cart. Someone took him.' She fought to keep back tears. 'Can't we find someone who was passing? Can't you make inquiries *now*?' She turned passionately to Folly. 'All you do is to stand there and do nothing; everyone ought to be looking for him, everyone——'

A voice came over a loud-speaker, not far away.

'Attention, everybody, attention please. Will any man or woman who saw a child, dressed in a blue woollen suit, sitting in a small push cart outside Lang's the drapers, between eleven-thirty and twelve o'clock please communicate with the police at once, at the police station or by telephone—Malling 11. Attention everybody, attention please . . .'

Suddenly Angela was in Jim's arms, crying.

Colonel Maitland's car pulled up in the High Street at half-past twelve. The Colonel walked briskly into the police station and went straight up to Forrest's office. This time, no one warned Cunningham of the Chief's arrival, and he was talking on the telephone when Maitland entered.

'Yes, that's right . . . Dressed in a blue woollen suit. A photograph will be circulated as soon as we can get the copies run off . . . Gantry, and answers to the name of Tub . . . T-U-B, Tub. That's right. About half an hour ago. It might

128

be connected with the Coombs' murder ... Yes, thanks, goodbye.'

He replaced the receiver, and looked round with a start.

'Why, good morning, sir.'

'What's this about?' asked Maitland, sharply.

'It's the Gantrys' baby, sir, a boy aged two, who appears to have been kidnapped from outside a shop in Middle Street. We heard about it within twenty minutes of the disappearance, and we've put out a general call. Superintendent Folly is taking it seriously.'

'I see,' said Maitland.

'If it *is* a kidnapping case, sir, it rather upsets our theory,' said Cunningham unhappily.

'How have the parents taken it?' asked Maitland.

Cunningham did not answer immediately, but reflected that Maitland had reached the crucial point quicker than he would have expected. That being, according to himself and Folly, how the Gantrys' had taken the disappearance. Folly's first reaction had been that it *might* be a put up job. He was now with Mrs. Gantry, judging her reaction.

The door opened, and Folly came in. His silk scarf drooped; but otherwise he was as spry as ever.

'Good morning, sir. Has Cunningham told you the latest?'

'Yes. Have you seen Mrs. Gantry?'

Folly threw up his arms; the scarf dropped unheeded to the desk.

'I went prepared to find that she was putting on an act, but there's no question of that at all. I've just seen her off with her husband and a friend. I think we can put aside any idea that it might be a trick to mislead us.'

'I see,' said Maitland.

Folly sat down rather heavily. Pencils rolled, pens rolled, rubbers bounced, but as usual, total disaster was adroitly averted. The man's a magician, thought Maitland irritably.

Folly said: 'When we first heard of this, we were putting the finishing touches to a report. I wouldn't say that this development makes the report so much waste paper, but it does upset it in some respects. We've been concentrating rather on the Gantrys'.'

'Let me hear it,' Maitland invited.

129

Folly carefully set one set of pink fingers against the other set of pink fingers and said equably: 'Go ahead, Cunningham.'

Had Lecky and Jim been able to hear the report which Cunningham read to the Chief Constable, Lecky would have been in high delight and Jim cast down to a deeper depression. Lecky's careful assessment of the situation was repeated; his inferences from everything that had happened were practically the same as those which Folly and Cunningham had drawn. Presented in Cunningham's quiet voice, the case seemed overwhelming, the issue hardly in doubt: the Langfords and the Gantrys were conspiring together.

'The one thing we haven't yet got, sir, is evidence that the Gantrys and the Langfords are old acquaintances,' said Cunningham, 'and I'm trying to get something on those lines now. We don't say that we've got an unbreakable case, of course, but there is a lot of circumstantial evidence.'

'So I see,' said Maitland drily. 'Is there anything else?'

'The only other motive we know of is Dale's,' said Cunningham. 'He does take over the whole of the business, but as it was destroyed by fire and he's in a terrible mess, the bottom seems to have been knocked out of that. There's the fact that he was nearly lost in the fire, too. If he himself started it—which seems most unlikely—he would hardly have allowed himself to be trapped.'

'No,' agreed Maitland.

'There is another thing, sir,' said Cunningham. 'Andrew Dale is wealthy in his own right. He inherited a fortune from his father. His only motive, I think, would be gain—and he doesn't need money. Moreover, Mr. Coombs was thinking of retiring from any active part in the business in the near future. So Dale had only a matter of months to wait before assuming complete control of the firm.'

Maitland pondered for a few moments, and then asked:

'What about this market salesman O'Hara talked about?'

'We've been working on him, sir,' said Cunningham. 'Such a man undoubtedly exists. Our men on duty in the market place remember him, and he wasn't unlike O'Hara in build, while both had ginger hair. He must have had a hawker's licence, but we've got no dossier about him. The people at the cooked meat stall near which he had his pitch, know him fairly well. His name was "Syd"—that's the best we can get, sir. He brought a lot of oddments for sale, the kind of things which might have been stolen. He also did a good trade in combs and cheap hosiery. He rarely stayed after midday. O'Hara is known to have bought goods from him,' Cunningham added. 'Undoubtedly it bears out O'Hara's story. On the other hand, he and O'Hara might have worked together. We shan't know until we've picked up the man.'

'What about this dark-haired chap who was seen at the Gantrys' house?'

'No trace at all, I'm afraid, sir.'

'And the car? You got half the number, didn't you?'

'Rather more than half,' said Cunningham. 'At least, Sergeant Owen did. No car with that number was seen on the day in question. I'm afraid we shall have to assume that the number plates were false. The car was a Wolseley, a fairly late model. It isn't an uncommon car, sir, and there are at least thirty owned in Malling and the surrounding district. But there is one curious thing, arising from our inquiries.'

'And what is that?'

'Porton, the bookmaker, owns one, and it was he who testified to O'Hara's gambling successes,' said Cunningham. 'True, he's shown us the books and the entries are there all right, and yet if Porton is concerned, it's the kind of thing he would arrange so that O'Hara could explain where he got the money with which to make his purchases.'

'Hmm. Do you really think that Porton is involved?'

'I find it hard to believe,' admitted Cunningham. 'He's been here for so long, and he's a wealthy man. The truth is, sir, that *I'm* completely beaten. The case was building up nicely against the Gantrys, but this morning's business makes a big difference.'

Maitland looked at Folly.

'And how do you feel about it?'

Folly smiled faintly. 'Very much the same as Cunningham,' he admitted. 'I can't say that I see anything more than Cunningham does, at the moment, but I am a little puzzled by one thing he hasn't mentioned.'

'And that is?'

131

Folly said: 'The *Record* man, Lecky. I've known him for years. He's often worked on cases in which I've been concerned, and yet—he seems to turn up everywhere in this case. It's almost uncanny.' For Folly to express himself so strongly was most unusual. 'Even this morning, he arrived as soon as my man came in to report the disappearance of the Gantry child. He was able to tell us what the child was wearing, almost as if he knew beforehand that there would be a search for him. I certainly wouldn't suggest that Lecky is involved, and yet——'

He broke off.

Maitland said: 'Well?'

'Last night, Lecky was waiting outside Dr. Lawson's house. He met Gantry, and drove him home,' said Jolly. 'If Gantry is involved, we've a new slant on Lecky. He and Gantry say that they hadn't met until this case began, but they were seen having lunch in the Malling Restaurant on the day we arrested O'Hara. In fact they were lunching together when Lecky hurried across to speak to you, as you left the office. Perhaps you remember him?'

'Yes, I do,' said Maitland. 'What was Lawson's report?'

Cunningham looked disgusted. 'He won't commit himself to any opinion yet,' he said. 'He's going to London this afternoon, and promises to have a word with Langford's London doctor. We got the name of the doctor from Andrew Dale.'

'I see,' said Maitland. 'Is there anything else?'

'Nothing more to report,' Folly said. 'I am checking on Porton, trying to discover whether he did go to Newmarket for those two days or whether he was somewhere else. He has several offices, including one in London, and I'm finding out whether anything is known against him outside Malling. I'm still searching for the will, too.'

'Is there no trace of it at all?' asked Maitland.

'None. We're going through the charred papers at the burned-out office,' Folly told him. 'There is also the possibility that Mrs. Gantry collected something from Mrs. Dale. I think the attempt to get that "something" explains the attack on her, and it could be that the kidnapping of the child is an attempt to blackmail the Gantrys into parting with it. Of course, that means that either Dale or his mother are somehow involved.

132

The case is full of odd twists and loose ends.'

'And further complicated by the relationship of Dale and Mrs. Langford,' observed Maitland. He stood up. Well, I know you're doing all you can. Only one thing appears to need emphasis. Quite the most important thing now is to find the Gantrys' child.'

CHAPTER FIFTEEN

NO NEWS OF TUB

Not until she was walking up the drive of the house did Angela remember that Marjorie had gone off to look for Tub, and had not returned. She told Jim, who immediately went to see Paddy. He did not want Paddy to be told of what had happened for a little while, because he would only harrow Angela's feelings.

'Paddy,' he said abruptly, 'there's a taxi waiting outside. Go to the end of Middle Street, and look for Mrs. Langford. Tell her we're back here. Tell her that nothing has been found, and ask her to say nothing until she's discussed it with us again.'

Not unnaturally, Paddy looked mystified.

'Hurry, please,' said Jim, sharply.

'Sure and I can't go any faster than I am doing,' said Paddy, annoyed. 'Does it matter if the casserole isn't done properly or the potatoes are boiling over? Certainly it doesn't matter, I'll leave them to ye.'

He took off his apron and marched out.

He was halfway up the drive, when Angela said:

'Jim, you ought to tell him. He'll only find out from someone else, and it will be a shock to him.'

'Paddy!' cried Jim, and went hurrying down the drive.

There was something in his voice and his expression that brought a change in Paddy O'Hara, and he stopped suddenly.

'Tub's lost.'

'What are ye saying?' asked Paddy, incredulously.

'Tub's lost. We're afraid he's been—kidnapped.' The word had taken on a new and sinister meaning.

Paddy stared. 'Do ye mean to tell me——'

'Yes, Tub's lost,' Jim repeated. 'Paddy, I want to be alone with Mrs. Gantry for half an hour, and that's why I want you

134

to go to Mrs. Langford. She's searching for Tub. So are the police. We're doing everything we can.'

'But it doesn't make sense,' said Paddy.

'No,' admitted Jim, 'it doesn't make sense, but it's happened. Just bring Mrs. Langford back here, will you? It doesn't matter about the message.'

Paddy said: 'Are ye standing there and telling me, Mr. Gantry, that *Tub's* been taken away by some miserable blackguard! Tub—b'God, if they harm a hair of his head it's answering to Paddy O'Hara they'll be! I'll murder them! I'll tear them to bits, that I will.' His eyes were glittering and his words were jumbled, he was beside himself. 'I'm telling ye, Mr. Gantry——'

Jim said in a low-pitched voice: 'Find Mrs. Langford, Paddy.'

Without another word, Paddy turned on his heel.

Jim went back to the house.

Angela was standing in the hall. Her face was still very pale, but she was composed enough now.

Jim thought it might be better to leave her for a few minutes on her own. She went towards the kitchen. He looked after her and saw her mechanical movements, her drawn face. She looked much older. He turned away quickly. It wouldn't be wise to let her be alone too long.

He gave her about fifteen minutes and then ambled into the kitchen. Angela was turning the gas down under the potatoes. She did not notice that the gas had gone out. Without speaking, Jim lit it again.

Angela went to the sink; and suddenly her shoulders began to heave. A lump came into Jim's throat. It was so futile to pretend that Tub might come back at any moment. Angela was convinced that his disappearance was connected with the crimes: so was he.

Angela blew her nose, and said: 'I can't go on like this, I must do something.'

'Didn't Mrs. Allison say that she thought there was something you could do?' Jim asked.

'Yes. No. Oh, I don't know. I hardly heard half of what she was saying.' She turned to face him. 'Darling, I *can't* just stand here and look after the meals and the house and behave as if everything were normal. I keep thinking I can hear Tub. He seems to be everywhere. I must *do* something. Darling, find me something to do!'

Jim said: 'First, we're going to have lunch. No nonsense, you're going to eat. Then we'll start on something.'

'*Damn lunch!*' cried Angela. 'I couldn't eat if you tried to force it down me!' She picked up a saucepan lid and flung it on the floor. It clattered and rolled against the wall. Next moment, there were tears in her eyes and she was in his arms. 'Jim, don't let me behave like this. It makes me so ashamed.'

'Let's get this cooking finished, and try to eat,' he said, practically.

He did not want to sit at the table with George and Marjorie. He found himself unreasonably blaming them. If they hadn't come, this would never have happened. It wasn't fair, but he hated the thought of eating with them. He might say something silly. George was in a difficult enough position already. He must be careful. Angela probably felt much the same as he did.

'Hallo,' called George, from the door.

They both swung round. He stood there, smiling, quite unaware of what had happened, but his expression altered when he saw their faces. He looked hard at Angela, then at Jim, and his voice sharpened.

'Has anything gone wrong?'

Angela said: 'Tub—they've taken Tub.'

'*They've taken Tub?*' echoed George, in bewilderment.

'Yes. Stolen him. *Kidnapped* him,' said Angela. Words tumbled out of her. There was something about George; he was the kind of man in whom one could not help confiding. There was a fount of sympathy and understanding in him, perhaps because he had suffered so much.

'I wonder how I can help,' said George, quietly. 'There must be something we can do.'

'That's what I've been saying,' said Angela. 'All Jim seems to want to do is eat!' She sent a quick, natural smile at Jim.

'Well, that won't do you any harm,' George said. 'Did you say that Marjorie is still out looking for him?'

By the time Angela had explained what had happened in Malling, there was a ring at the front door bell. George said:

'I expect that's her,' and turned to go out. There was a pause, and then they heard Andrew Dale's voice.

'Hallo, George. Are Jim and Angela in?'

Angela said quickly: 'I don't think I want to talk to Andrew, darling.'

'I'll see him,' said Jim. He went out, finding Andrew standing on the threshold of the living-room and George about to come to the kitchen.

Andrew said: 'Jim, I'm terribly sorry about this.'

'I know you are, old chap.'

'I came out as soon as I heard,' Andrew said. 'What I want to do is to help. There isn't much I can do, except keep on at the police. Of course, you mustn't rule out the possibility that he's wandering around somewhere, you know.'

Jim said hopelessly: 'It's a possibility, but a fairly remote one.'

'Could be, but there's a chance. I can tell you one thing. The police have been in touch with all the hospitals and nursing-homes in the town, so it's not a question of an accident.'

Jim said quickly: 'That's good to hear. I had a sneaking fear that it might be something like that. I don't think Angela had thought of it.'

He turned, to go and tell her. They had decided not to wait lunch for Marjorie, and Angela was coming from the kitchen with a pile of plates.

'Hallo, Andrew,' she smiled.

'It's so difficult to know what to say,' said Andrew. 'I've come to tell you that I'll gladly drop everything and try to help, if there's anything at all you think I can do.'

He was looking much better than on the previous day. His eyes were bright, and the haggard look had gone from his face.

Jim's eyes flickered to George.

These two men were in love with the same woman, and the situation was full of difficulties. Now, they appeared to forget everything in their concern for Tub. Jim detected no sign at all of bitterness in George. Nothing Andrew said or did indicated his true feelings for Marjorie.

The telephone rang.

137

Angela, who had been pecking at her food, dropped her fork and rushed into the hall. When she lifted the receiver, all three men were behind her.

'Yes, this is Malling 331,' she said. 'Yes ... *Oh.*'

The disappointment in her voice was heart-breaking.

'It's Lecky,' she said, and handed the receiver to Jim.

'Hallo, Lecky,' said Jim, sharply. 'What is it?'

Lecky, too, was crisp. 'I've just been talking to your man, O'Hara. He tells me you sent him to look for Mrs. Langford.'

'That's right.'

'Has Mrs. Langford come back yet?'

'No.'

'Well, I was speaking to our local man half an hour ago,' said Lecky. 'He says that he saw Mrs. Langford in a car heading south, about a quarter to one. She was in the back of the car, a Wolseley. A Wolseley was mentioned once before, wasn't it?'

Jim gave a startled exclamation.

'I thought you ought to know about it,' said Lecky. 'I've told the police, of course. They'll probably be along soon to see what you can tell them. With Langford staying there, I thought it might be a bit of a shock to him if the police tackled him first. Sorry to put more trouble on your shoulders.'

'I appreciate——'

Lecky said quickly: 'The front page of the *Record* will carry a picture of Tub in the morning, old chap. You need all publicity possible, and I'll see you get it. 'Bye.'

He rang off.

The others had followed Angela back into the dining-room. The men had finished, Andrew was sitting with a glass of cider in front of him.

'I suppose he was out for news,' he said.

Jim said: 'He wasn't, as a matter of fact. He told me a rather queer thing.' He was acutely conscious of the awkwardness of the situation. It would not have been so bad had George been alone, but what would Andrew's reaction be when he heard that Marjorie had been seen driving out of town?

Jim said hurriedly: 'Apparently the local correspondent of the *Record* thinks he saw Marjorie being driven out of town in a Wolseley, a little while after she had left Angela. I can't

138

make head or tale of it, can you? Lecky thought we ought to know.'

George said: 'Why should she? He must have been mistaken.'

Andrew snapped: 'Why did he mention a Wolseley?'

'Apparently a Wolseley was used the other day,' said Jim, and then added thoughtfully: 'Damn it, of course it was a Wolseley which took the dark-haired customer away from the end of the road. I'm inclined to agree with George, there must have been a mistake.'

Andrew said: 'If anything has happened to Marjorie——'

'Nothing can have happened!' exclaimed George.

What a nightmare this was! Jim looked helplessly from one man to the other. Angela had given up all pretence at eating. There was a moment of silence, and then George and Andrew both started to talk at once. At the same time a car drew up outside, and Paddy came hurrying along the drive, his face set. He had no news.

Jim went out to see him.

'I couldn't find her,' Paddy said fiercely, 'and they haven't found Tub. It's a useless lot of fools the police are. They should have found him by now. If I could get behind them I would make them do something, so I would!'

'Paddy, they're doing everything they can.'

'Och, but it's not enough,' cried Paddy. 'It's God's help we need, and the help of men who know what they're doing.' He stormed off towards the kitchen. As he did so two cars pulled up.

One thing after another, Jim thought wearily, recognising Folly and Cunningham in the first and Mrs. Allison in the second.

Angela left the police with the three men, and went with Mrs. Allison into the sitting-room. Folly was friendly enough. Lecky had told him about Marjorie, and he was anxious to know whether she had told George that she expected to go out of Malling that day.

'Of course she didn't expect to,' said George, 'she would have told me.'

'Does she know anyone at Canham?' asked Folly, mentioning the town immediately south of Malling.

'No.'

'Or anyone in that direction?'

'No,' answered George, 'and if my wife left Malling this morning, she did not do so of her own free will, I'm sure of that.'

Jim thought: Can *Marjorie* have been kidnapped? The idea seemed absurd. Then he heard Andrew saying:

'... of course, I may be wrong, but it is possible and it would explain her going off, wouldn't it?'

'What would?' demanded Jim.

'Andrew thinks Marjorie may have seen Tub and managed to get someone to take her after him,' said George, looking worried. 'She might have picked up a taxi. Are there any Wolseleys used in private hire work in Malling, do you know?'

'Several,' Cunningham told him.

'Well, then, there's a chance,' said Andrew.

Cunningham said: 'We're checking up on all the Wolseleys, of course. Believe me, Mr. Gantry, we are doing everything we can. The fact that your son hasn't been found yet proves how right we were to take it seriously from the first. Our inquiries started within a few minutes of the report reaching us.'

'Thanks,' said Jim, in a dry voice.

Folly's natural exuberance, damped down by Tub's disappearance, began very slightly to rise. Cunningham watched expectantly, sensing the steel beneath the velvet glove, when Folly spoke in a voice that held the timbre of a gentle, hypnotic purr:

'Now, gentlemen, while all three of you are together, I know you will understand why I ask one question which has greatly worried me. That is, the fact that Mr. Coombs's will has not yet been found.'

'That's a statement, not a question,' Andrew said, with a faint smile.

Folly said silkily: 'Perhaps the splitting of hairs could be left till later, Mr. Dale? Splendid. A delightful pastime, but one unlikely to get us very far. Now, here's the question. Have any of you the slightest idea where the will might be?'

Had Lecky not told Jim what to expect of Folly, he would have been astonished at the question of the will being brought in at this stage. He judged, however, that Folly was still working on the possibility that he, George and Andrew were all concerned, and he was out to watch their reactions to the question while they were all together.

If this were so, Jim decided that he had been disappointed.

Andrew told him that Coombs had never mentioned a will to him, had never to his knowledge had a secret hiding place, and thought it likely that the will, if there had ever been one, had been burned. George said that he had not known Coombs well enough to be taken into his confidence, and certainly had no idea whether there was a will. Jim said that he would not have known there was any bother about a will had it not been mentioned in the *Record* the previous morning.

'Ahh,' said Folly, sitting back, his attitude that of a stout and replete man about to indulge in forty winks; then suddenly the eyelids flicked fully open, the eyes, small, shrewd and very bright, fixed themselves on Jim. 'What did Mrs. Gantry bring away from Mrs. Dale's house, Mr. Gantry?'

Jim leapt to his chair.

'Confound it, that's as good as calling my wife a liar!'

'What's all this about?' demanded Andrew. 'I heard that Angela had looked in, Jim, but it's the first time that I knew there was any talk of her bringing anything away.'

'The police seem to think she did,' said Jim. 'The simple truth is that she didn't. I'm afraid I take a poor view of this, Folly. I want my child back. You might concentrate on that.'

'I think the two crimes are connected,' Folly said gently.

He hoisted his considerable bulk neatly from the chair, and as he withdrew with Cunningham, the three men left there looked at each other in almost distrust. Folly had sown dissension; more, he had sown uneasiness.

Andrew said: 'Jim, why did Angela visit my mother?'

'Because your mother called here to see Marjorie, and Angela thought that by paying a return visit she might find out why,' answered Jim. 'It's as simple as that, whatever the police say. The fact that Angela was attacked and robbed immediately afterwards seems to have given them ideas.'

Andrew looked back at him thoughtfully.

'Our Council of War hasn't done much good,' said George.

The door opened as he spoke and Angela came in. To Jim's astonishment, she looked radiant. For a moment a wild hope

141

that there was news of Tub heartened him.

'Jim,' cried Angela, 'Mrs. Allison has had a marvellous idea. She's the President of the Women's Insitute. She's called an emergency meeting for this afternoon and invited all similar organisations, and they're going to search high and low for Tub. They're meeting at the Town Hall at three o'clock. Darling, I must go with them.' She broke off. It seemed that suddenly she realised that the search might be of little consequence. She had clutched at any straw, but, face to face with the three men, she realised how little they thought of it. 'Well, it's worth trying, anyhow,' she said in a muffled voice.

'Worth trying!' exclaimed Jim, and managed to put real feeling into his voice. 'It's a brainwave, darling—where is Mrs. Allison?' He hurried out into the hall, but as he glanced at Angela he knew that her momentary elation had gone. The scheme had only made her realise the sickening facts more clearly.

Then the telephone bell rang.

CHAPTER SIXTEEN

THE PUSH CART

'Are you going to answer it?' Andrew demanded testily.

Slowly Jim picked up the receiver. He heard Lecky saying with some impatience:

'Why the devil don't you answer? Is that you, Gantry? Listen to me. The police have found the push cart——'

'*What?*'

'It was in a ditch by the side of the Canham Road where it runs through Canham Forest,' said Lecky. 'The police are sending out a search-party at once. I thought you ought to know.'

Angela cried out: 'What is it? Jim, have they found him?'

Jim murmured a few words of thanks to Lecky, and put the receiver down. He turned to Angela, trying to keep his voice steady.

'No, but they think they've found the push cart.'

'Where?'

'In Canham Forest.'

'Canham *Forest!*' exclaimed Angela. 'Why, that's where——'

She turned and rushed upstairs. Mrs. Allison followed her.

'Are the police getting busy?' asked Andrew.

'Yes. That was Lecky. I——'

The telephone rang again. This time it was Cunningham, with the same news. By the time Jim had finished speaking to him, Angela was downstairs, wearing her coat and walking shoes.

'Mrs. Allison is going to drive us out,' she cried. 'Jim, hurry!'

'Will there be room for me?' asked Andrew, eagerly.

'And me?' asked George.

143

There appeared to be plenty of room, and they all hurried down the drive. As they were piling into the car, a cry came from the drive and Paddy came running towards them, calling as he ran.

'So ye wouldn't be waiting for me,' he gasped.

Andrew reopened the door, and Paddy squeezed himself in, settling on the floor between their feet.

Canham Forest was seven miles outside Malling, and most of the way was hilly ground. From the crest of the next hill, they could see a number of police cars in front of them. The forest stretched for miles in either direction, but there were several open spaces where the trees had been cut down.

Presently the first car slowed down. The others followed suit, but Mrs. Allison did not slacken speed; driving skilfully until she was second in the column. A little way ahead a policeman and two women were standing by the side of the road.

'There it is!' cried Angela.

They pulled out in front of the leading police car. On the grass verge was Tub's push cart. It was a sad sight. One wheel was buckled, the handle was broken, the seat splintered; but there was no doubt at all that it was Tub's.

Folly and Cunningham moved up silently.

'Are you sure that it is your son's cart?'

'Quite sure.' Jim pointed to some brass screws and small metal plates, to which the straps were fastened. 'I put those there myself. It's his cart all right.'

Angela caught her breath. 'How was it broken up?'

Police Constable Small joined the group.

'It wouldn't surprise me, sir, if it wasn't one of them accidents which weren't reported.'

Both Folly and Cunningham turned on him in silent fury, but the damage was done.

Jim, feeling more sick than ever, knew that this simple explanation might be the right one. Tub might have been run down while crossing the road. The driver of the car might have got out, put cart and Tub into the car and, here in the loneliness of the forest, tried to hide all traces of the accident.

Folly went on: 'Use your common sense, man! There is no sign of blood, nothing at all to suggest that the child was in it

144

when the cart was smashed.'

Angela clutched Jim's arm.

'And the child couldn't have got out of Malling,' Folly continued, 'if there had been an accident, it would have been in the town, with dozens of spectators.'

Of course, thought Jim. What a fool I was!

The police were marshalled, now, with Folly giving crisp instructions. They were to form up in two rows, seven men aside, and walk through the forest, making sure that all the ground was covered.

The Superintendent then turned his attention to the county policeman and the two women. In spite of the circumstances, Jim found himself admiring his manner with people who might easily have become nervous. Folly was friendly and encouraging, listening with no sign of impatience as the elder of the two women rambled through her story. It appeared that she and her daughter had been walking along the road, having missed one bus into Malling and knowing that another would not be along for an hour. They had seen something poking out of a ditch. It looked bright and new, and proved to be the red handle of the push-cart. Knowing of the small boy's disappearance they had put two and two together, and with commendable presence of mind stopped a cyclist and asked him to take the news to the village policeman.

Folly smiled his congratulations.

'Were you on duty on this road this morning?'

'Yes, sir, between half-past twelve and one.'

'Have you heard the inquiry about a Wolseley car?'

'Yes, sir. And called to mind what cars *did* pass. There weren't very many; it isn't a busy road except at weekends, sir. I remember two Wolseleys, both dark blue or black. I couldn't be sure which. One passed at about a quarter to one, the other after one o'clock—just when I was cycling home to my dinner, sir.'

'Did you notice the occupants?'

'I'm afraid I didn't,' said the policeman. 'I *think* a lady was in the back of one; that's all I can say for certain.'

'I see,' said Folly. 'You've done very well, Constable.'

'Thank you, sir.'

Jim looked away from the part of the forest in which the

police were searching. It was impossible to believe that they were looking for his son, for the *body* of his son.

Folly's questions went on, almost interminable. Where was the nearest house to this spot? Did the policeman or the women know of anyone who had driven, cycled or walked through the forest about midday? Their answers were vague. Jim realised the unlikelihood of getting news quickly. He almost wished that he and Angela had not come.

Then a policeman called out: 'What's that?'

It was as if an electric shock passed through them all. Everyone started, everyone turned to look towards the search party. Angela gripped Jim's arm.

A man moved across the uneven ground, bent down, and picked up something blue.

'*That's Tub's coat!*' cried Angela.

She raced towards the man, stumbling but keeping her balance. Several policemen concentrated their search near the spot where the woollen coat had been found. As Angela drew up, another man discovered the leggings of the woollen suit. Angela examined them feverishly, but there were no marks or indication of violence.

Folly took the coat and examined it closely. There were two small brownish stains on the front. He touched the surface with his fingernail; it was chocolate.

'I suppose he had chocolate while he was out with you?'

Angela shook her head.

'I never let him have chocolate when he's out; he makes such a mess.'

'Well, there it is,' said Folly with a gentle smile. 'I think we can say that whoever approached him offered the chocolate and Tub decided that he was a friend. The child was put into the car, driven out here and, to make sure that he wasn't recognised from his clothes or the cart, both were thrown out. Doesn't that sound likely, Mrs. Gantry?'

'It—yes, I suppose it does.'

'I think it proves one thing which will set your mind at rest,' said Folly. 'Tub's all right. He's come to no harm.'

'But——'

'I know we've got to find him,' went on Folly, 'but it's a relief to know that it wasn't an accident, isn't it? I doubt whether we'll find anything else here,' he added. 'If they'd wanted to turn him loose in the forest, they wouldn't have taken off his coat.'

'But you'll keep looking?'

'Yes, of course. That is, my men will. I'm going into the village. Sergeant Cunningham will go the other way, and we'll both try to find someone who saw the car when it pulled up here.' He spoke very simply. 'I don't really think it will be any good for you to stay, Mrs. Gantry. Do if you wish, of course, but this kind of inquiry is a tedious and time-taking one, you know. I'll telephone you the moment I've any news.'

'I know you will,' said Angela, 'but——'

Mrs. Allison said: 'It seems certain that they took him towards Canham. Would you rather go there, Mrs. Gantry?'

'Oh yes!' cried Angela.

They all piled back into the car except Paddy who decided to stay.

Driving away, Angela said in a small voice: 'I suppose Folly is right, really. There isn't much chance of us finding anything, if the police can't.'

'We might have some luck,' said George.

Something in the tone of his voice made Jim look at him sharply. George, of course, had as much reason to be anxious as he and Angela. Marjorie had been seen travelling along this road; she might also have been forced to go against her will.

And she might have come of her own accord. *She might even be concerned in the kidnapping.*

That thought came as a shock, and Jim began to brood over it. Chocolate was the kind of bribe which would be offered to a child, and Marjorie had known that Tub was extremely fond of it. And Tub, although a friendly child, was normally distrustful of strangers outside the house. If someone who he knew had taken him away——

But Marjorie had been in the shop, with Angela.

They drove through the forest and then across flat country. Soon, they were driving through the outskirts of Canham. It was little more than a large village, it's only useful purpose being that it was a market town.

The High Street was wide and not unattractive. Halfway down they came to The George Hotel; and outside the hotel

147

was a small car.

Mrs. Allison pulled up immediately behind it.

'I suppose there is some point in being here,' said Angela, wearily.

'We'll have a cup of tea,' said George.

Jim was frowning at the little car in front of them.

'I think I know that car,' he said. 'It's Lecky's, or it's very much like Lecky's.'

The door of the hotel opened suddenly and Lecky appeared. Seeing them he pointed urgently towards the far end of the High Street.

'He wants us to go further along,' Mrs. Allison remarked.

'Infernal nerve!' exclaimed Andrew.

'For the love of Mike, go away!' hissed Lecky. *'I'll send a message, to the Antelope. Hurry!'*

He turned and disappeared.

'I don't see why we should take any notice of what he says,' protested Andrew. 'The fellow thinks he's the cat's whiskers, but——'

The protest was in vain, for Mrs. Allison was already driving off. A little way along the High Street narrowed. There was a T junction and, facing them, a smaller hotel with a stone antelope over the porch. Once again Mrs. Allison made her own decision, and soon a bewildered party stood in the car park at the back of the hotel.

Andrew was still annoyed with Lecky, and said so.

'Well, he has always got results,' Jim commented.

'I expect he'll send word,' observed George. 'We'd better go in and have some tea.'

It was a little after half-past three. The old building with its oak beams and low ceilings had an olde-worlde air that was both authentic and soothing. A maid came for their order. Mrs. Allison gave it. She seemed to be in complete control of the party, steadying them all with her calm commonsense.

'I feel so much happier now,' she said. 'I was so afraid that Tub had met with an accident.'

As she spoke, the door opened and Lecky burst in.

He looked furiously angry as he strode towards them. They sat round the fireplace, looking up at him in some alarm.

'I hope you're all satisfied with yourselves,' he snarled. 'I hope you're pleased that——'

Andrew snapped: 'Who the devil do you think you're addressing, Lecky?'

'One fool for a start,' growled Lecky. He flung himself into a chair. 'But it's enough to make a saint swear! The way I've worked to try to find out something, and then you arrive when I'm getting somewhere. If you'd been a quarter of an hour later, it wouldn't have mattered. They saw you, of course, and cleared off immediately.'

'Who the devil are they?' demanded Andrew.

'Bookmaker Porton and his clerk,' answered Lecky, and lit a cigarette. 'Yes, *Porton*. In a Wolseley. I've discovered a thing or two about Porton. He's quite a boy in his own way, and he doesn't make money out of racing only. He owns two or three fleets of taxis in seaside towns near here, *and the cars are all Wolseleys.*'

'Do the police know?' demanded Andrew, sharply.

'If they don't they ought to,' retorted Lecky. 'Folly won't be long in finding out. Porton himself drove out here in a Packard just after I'd telephoned you, Gantry. I thought I would try to catch up with him. I did, and you——' He shrugged his shoulders. 'Well, you didn't know what you were doing, I mustn't be too hard on you. I was about to hear plenty, though.'

'Is this just guesswork, or have you got something against Porton?' asked Jim.

'There are two or three *very* odd things about Porton,' said Lecky. 'I don't know whether the police have discovered them yet. One of his tic-tac men is ginger-haired, about O'Hara's size, and another is small and dark with a pale face. Curious facts, aren't they?'

'Are you sure about this?' demanded George.

'Pretty sure.'

'You can't be sure that they're the same men,' Jim objected. 'I mean, the men who broke into the house.'

'I wouldn't like to bet that they aren't,' said Lecky. 'That isn't all, either. There are one or two things which I want to keep to myself for a little while.'

'Now look here, Lecky,' began Andrew, only to be interrupted by the waitress, who brought their tea.

'The same for me, please,' Lecky said with a grin.

'Yes, sir.' The girl put the things on the table and went out.

'Look here, Lecky,' Andrew began again, in a reasoning voice, 'I know you're pretty fly, you wouldn't be the star reporter of *The Record* if you weren't, but you're playing a dangerous game, you know.'

'How come?' asked Lecky.

'If you keep information back from the police so as to score a triumph for yourself, they might come down on you for withholding material evidence. Folly's got a reputation for being pretty severe if he thinks outsiders are butting in—but I expect you know that as well as I do.'

Lecky laughed.

'I do. But Folly's not vindictive. He wouldn't spare me or anyone else if he thought we were playing the fool, but I'm *not* playing the fool. You can't stop a man thinking and you can't stop a man from drawing his own conclusions, and what's more, you certainly can't stop a newspaperman from trying to prove that his conclusions are right! If I get material evidence I'll contact Folly in two shakes of a lamb's tail! One, actually.'

Andrew laughed. 'You're pretty sure of yourself.'

'Of course I am,' said Lecky. 'I have to be.' He looked round the room, and added: 'I'm glad this place is empty. I had a feeling that I was followed from the George.'

'I suppose your imagination couldn't be running away with you,' teased Andrew.

'Oh, it could,' admitted Lecky. Nevertheless, he got up and strolled towards the window, which overlooked the car-park. The others watched him. Jim noticed that he was careful to keep in a position where he could not be seen from outside.

Lecky reached the window and peered out from behind the curtains.

'Oh, stop play-acting,' snapped Andrew.

Lecky was staring fixedly into the car-park. He said in a low voice: 'Gantry, will you come over here?' As Jim got up, Lecky added: 'You'd recognise the dark-haired fellow again, wouldn't you?'

'Yes,' said Jim.

He approached as cautiously as Lecky had done. The others

sat watching. Jim looked out. He could see a man standing between two cars—a man who had the bonnet of one car up, and was doing something to the engine. It dawned on him that the man was interfering with Mrs. Allison's car.

All he could see of the man was his back and his dark hair.

He whispered: 'Andrew, go round to the car-park, someone is tampering with Mrs. Allison's car. Do you know if there's another way out?' he added to Lecky. 'We'll get him if we approached from both sides at once.'

CHAPTER SEVENTEEN

THE DARK-HAIRED MAN

Andrew was already at the door. The maid came in, and there was a clatter of crockery as Andrew pushed past her.

Lecky reached her side quickly.

'Is there a back way out?' he demanded. 'One to the car-park?'

'Only through the kitchen, sir, and that——'

'Where's the kitchen?'

'Next to the dining-room, but——'

Lecky hurried out. Jim and George followed. Andrew was still in the hall, and Lecky called: 'Give us two minutes, Dale.' Then he led the way into the kitchen, passing two startled waitresses. The others followed.

'Turn right, I think,' said Lecky.

They hurried along a passage, and saw the car-park immediately in front of them. The dark-haired man was moving away from the Austin. He glanced nervously about him, but they were hidden from him by a small car.

Jim whispered: *'It's the same man.'*

Then Andrew appeared at the corner of the hotel. His head showed only for a moment, but the dark-haired man spotted him. He turned, and saw Lecky. In a flash, he darted between two cars. Jim, following Lecky, saw their quarry leap over the bonnet of a car. Lecky tried to follow but slipped and fell to the ground. As Jim stumbled over him, George slipped past them and took the lead.

Lecky shouted: 'Go round to the back, Dale. The other side!'

Jim did not know whether Andrew obeyed. The dark-haired man was now in what looked like a builder's yard. There was a huge galvanised iron shed, with a small door. He disappeared into it and George followed. Jim went in after them.

There appeared to be another door at the other end, and groping their way towards this, George and Jim presently emerged.

Jim looked right and left but could see no sign of the man they were chasing. He hurried towards a gateway leading into the road at the side of the Antelope. Andrew and Lecky would surely have made certain that he did not escape in the other direction.

A brewer's dray was passing. No one else was in sight.

Jim called: 'Have you seen anyone running along here?'

'No, sir,' answered the driver cheerfully, 'not a soul.' His philosophy seemed to be that all men were mad, and Jim no madder than the rest.

Feeling rather a fool Jim stood looking along the street.

There was a high brick wall further along the road, a hedge and meadows on either side. He climbed up a bank so that he could see for miles, but there was no sign of a human being.

Disconsolate, he went back to the Antelope.

Angela exclaimed: 'What on earth have you been doing?'

'Why, what do you think I've been doing?' retorted Jim with as much dignity as he could muster.

'Well,' said Angela with wifely forthrightness, 'chasing bandits certainly doesn't seem to be your line. You've an enormous cobweb dangling behind your ear and your face is filthy.'

In silence Jim sought out the hotel bathroom. Angela was right, he thought, grimly scrubbing away, this was the second, or was it the third, time a quarry had escaped him.

Back in the hotel lounge, he met Andrew and George returning from the chase.

'Any luck?' Andrew demanded.

'No. Where's Lecky?'

'No idea, I expect he'll limp in soon and blame me for everything.'

'Well, the man did see you first,' declared George.

'I don't see how he could have,' objected Andrew.

'We all did our best,' Jim said, gruffly. 'You need a wash and brush up, George. I'll show you where the cloakroom is.'

Soon they were having tea, all of them on edge, looking up whenever there were footsteps in the hall. Two elderly couples came in, but there was no sign of Lecky. They waited for half an hour after finishing tea, and then Mrs. Allison said practically:

'There isn't much point in waiting. We'd better go.'

Jim thought miserably that it had been a wasted afternoon. What was worse, the Malling police did not know where they were and could not send any news of Tub.

They made their way to the car-park, Mrs. Allison and Angela a little ahead of the men. A child started to cry, and Angela's lips set tightly as she turned away.

Then she exclaimed: *'Oh!'*

There was something in the sound of her voice which startled Jim. She was staring downwards. So was Mrs. Allison, who stood with her hand outstretched, perfectly still.

A man was lying between the car and the wall.

Near him was a long-handled hammer.

Jim brushed past Angela. He recognised Lecky at once. There was an ugly wound in the back of his head.

Jim said hurriedly: 'Get a doctor,' but he knew that a doctor could do nothing. The newspaperman was dead.

At half-past five that afternoon, Folly and Cunningham were going through the dozens of reports which had come in since they had left for Canham Forest. Tub appeared to have been seen in almost every town in the British Isles. Nothing more had been discovered at Canham Forest or in the village. No one appeared to have been about at midday. The driver of the Wolseley had chosen a good spot and been lucky.

Cunningham pushed the papers aside in disgust.

'We're getting nowhere,' he said.

Folly said equably: 'It's often the way, laddie—the darkest hour before the dawn, and all that.'

'I hope you're right,' growled Cunningham.

'One line we'll have to follow again is Porton and his fleets of taxis,' Folly said. 'We haven't paid as much attention to them as we should have done. He left in the Packard just after one-fifteen, didn't he?'

'Yes, heading north.'

'He could have gone north and then turned back on the Canham Road,' remarked Folly. 'We'll have to have that

154

checked.'

Cunningham said: 'Our fellows will be going round in circles before the day's out.'

'An estimable exercise for the deflation of the ego,' said Folly, 'though not to be carried to excess.' He fumbled for a moment in the top drawer of his desk. 'I have here a little box of *pâté de foie gras* sandwiches. There comes a time when sustenance is not so much an indulgence as a necessity. That time is here and now.'

Cunningham looked on at the careful unveiling of the sandwiches with a certain suspicion.

'No cheese? No sardine?'

'Certainly not, dear boy. Cheese and sardine, though not to be despised in emergencies, do little to encourage one's taste for the more recherché joys of the table.'

He was in the middle of his third cup of coffee when the telephone rang.

Cunningham picked up the receiver, listened a few moments, then turned desperate eyes on Folly.

'Report from Canham. Lecky's been murdered.'

Folly flicked an errant crumb from his waistcoat, put his cup carefully back on the tray and rose majestically to his feet.

They were at Canham soon after six o'clock. The local police were then in charge, and two doctors had seen Lecky, whose body had been taken into the hotel. Folly wished it had not been moved. The local constable said, with pride, that ne had taken photographs, there wasn't anything to worry about in that respect. Absently, Folly congratulated him. He began to ask questions, sitting in a small room set aside for the police by the hotel manager. The whole story came out, including Lecky's remarks about Porton. Cunningham made notes.

Questioned, Andrew replied that Lecky had rushed past him, towards the side of the Antelope, while he himself had followed Jim and George towards the builder's yard. Seeing their plight, he had turned to follow Lecky, but had not caught sight of him. Nor had he seen the dark-haired man. Between the moment when the party had entered the car-park and that when Lecky's body had been discovered, the murder had been committed.

155

'It seems to me,' said George, in his calm way, 'that the man managed to hide himself in the car-park again. Lecky probably heard or saw him and started to close in, poor chap.'

Folly's manner was bland but non-committal.

The first thing he discovered outside was that two plugs of Mrs. Allison's car had been loosened. The local policeman explained, quite unnecessarily, that it was obviously the work of the dark-haired man, the object being to delay the party.

It was two hours before they got back to Malling. Mrs. Allison drove back to Bligh Avenue, Cunningham and Folly went straight to the police station. Folly had been very quiet on the journey, and Cunningham looked at him curiously but did not press him to talk.

In the office, Folly said: 'Have you noticed anything queer about the stories we've heard, Cunningham?'

'In what particular way?' asked Cunningham. When Folly did not immediately answer, he went on: 'It's odd that they all separated, isn't it?'

'That's the point,' said Folly, approvingly. 'It's natural enough that they split up, but surprising that they were so long getting together again. We can't be sure of a single one of them.'

'Not of the two women?' asked Cunningham, surprised.

'No,' said Folly, 'and we mustn't allow ourselves to assume that a woman couldn't have killed Lecky. It was done with a long-handled hammer, not particularly heavy, with a polished surface. The surface was wiped clean of prints. A woman could have swung it easily enough. At first, it looked as if Lecky had been stalking his quarry, but I doubt whether he was.'

'Then what do you think he was doing?'

'Looking at Mrs. Allison's car, which the dark-haired man had been tampering with,' Folly said. 'Two plugs were loose—presumably the man tried to take the plugs away and so delay them. We needn't waste time wondering why. Let's look at the facts as they're generally agreed among them all. After the first rush, they lost their quarry. The three men went off, on their own—each going in a different direction. The two women were left in the hotel. For five minutes Mrs. Allison was in the cloakroom, so the women were separated for that

156

five minutes. Not one of them can give an alibi for *any* of the others.

'Five minutes would have been ample time,' went on Folly. 'Let us suppose that Lecky decided that the chase was hopeless, and went back to the car. He was the most practical of the lot. His first move would be to find out if anything was wrong with it. He would lift the bonnet and look. He could be seen from the lounge window and from both ends of the car-park. Absorbed in his investigation, he might easily have been approached unobserved. One swing with the hammer was enough to break his skull. All that the murderer had to do was to wipe the handle clean and get away. If it was one of the men, it could have been done before entering the hotel. If one of the women, she could have slipped out and back again in the five minutes during which we know they were separated.'

Cunningham said slowly: 'You're right, of course.' He hesitated. 'Is there any point in including Mrs. Allison?'

'I think so. Remember that she was near at hand when Mrs. Gantry was first attacked. We certainly can't rule her out. Still, we can say with some confidence why the murder was committed.'

'Why?' asked Cunningham. 'Oh, I see. You mean that Lecky had said that he knew something about Porton and that he suspected other things which he couldn't yet prove. So any one of them, afraid that he had discovered too much, might have taken the first chance of getting rid of him.'

Folly nodded.

Paddy met the returning party at the house. His face dropped when he saw their expressions, and without a word he turned and went inside. Andrew stayed for only a few minutes. Mrs. Allison offered to drive him home, and George, Angela and Jim watched them drive off.

George spoke first. 'She's very helpful, isn't she?'

'I don't know what I would have done without her,' Angela said. 'She's been marvellous. Nothing makes her turn a hair—she's rather like you, George.'

'I'm feeling like turning a lot of hairs at the moment,' George said grimly, and then burst out with unusual feeling: 'What can have happened to Marjorie? Where is she? The police seem to think that she went off with Tub, but that's absurd!'

'We'll hear something soon,' Jim said reassuringly. 'If you two will take my advice, you'll go and lie down for a bit. You look tired out, George, and Angela looks as if she hasn't slept for a week.'

George said quietly: 'Perhaps you're right.'

Angela watched him go upstairs, then leaned back and closed her eyes. Jim stared out into the darkness. He could not think clearly, because he could hear Tub's voice in his ears all the time. Suddenly, he got up. Angela had dropped into a doze, and did not stir. He went upstairs to the nursery. The cot was ready, neat and clean.

Blindly, he turned away.

He was halfway down the stairs when the telephone rang. Paddy was speaking into it before Jim reached the hall. Jim hurried forward, as Paddy said:

'Yes, hold on will ye?' and then put his hand over the mouth-piece and exclaimed: ' 'Tis Mrs. Langford, asking for ye!'

CHAPTER EIGHTEEN

'INVITATION'

Jim's heart was thumping as he picked up the receiver, and said: 'Hallo, Marjorie.' She did not immediately reply. There was a mutter of voices in the background.

The sitting-room door opened. Angela stood watching him, and Paddy moved across to her.

'Hallo, Marjorie,' repeated Jim.

'Jim.' She sounded breathless. 'Jim, I've only got a moment. You and Angela must come to Canport tonight. It's about Tub. He's all right, but——'

She broke off. The murmur of voices continued. Jim glanced at Angela, and called: 'Tub's all right, but we haven't found him yet.' He hardly knew what he wanted to say to her, he was so desperately anxious not to raise her hopes too high. 'Are you there, Marjorie?' he demanded.

'Yes. Jim, listen. You're not to tell the police. You're not to tell anyone. Come to Canport and wait outside the Red Lion. Did you get that?'

'Canport, Red Lion,' said Jim. 'What time?'

'You must be there by ten o'clock,' said Marjorie. 'Jim, don't forget, *no* one else must know——'

'We'll have to come by taxi, the driver will have to know.'

There was a murmur of voices in the background. A man's voice sounded loud for a moment, then faded.

'You mustn't tell him where you're going,' Marjorie said at last. 'The driver, I mean. Don't tell George, either, unless he's coming with you.'

'I see,' said Jim. 'Why should we come, Marjorie?'

'You must! Jim, for Tub's sake——'

She rang off.

Jim turned from the telephone. Angela stood looking at him,

159

her eyes enormous.

'For the love of St. Peter, what did she say?' cried Paddy.

Jim said: 'She assured me that Tub is all right. Mrs. Gantry and I have to go out tonight, Paddy.'

'Where will ye be going?'

'I'm not quite sure, yet,' said Jim. 'We'll meet someone on the road who will tell us.'

The lie came smoothly. He had not had time to think, and the last person in whom to repose a confidence of such a nature was Paddy. Grumbling angrily, he stamped off towards the kitchen.

Angela insisted tensely: 'What did she *say*, Jim?'

'She told me Tub was all right,' said Jim, 'and that we were to go to Canport tonight, getting there at ten o'clock. That means we'll have to leave in twenty minutes. We aren't to tell anyone except George, and only then if he is coming with us. There was someone with Marjorie——'

'But how on earth can we get to Canport tonight *without* telling someone?' demanded Angela. 'It's fifteen miles the other side of Canham.'

Jim said: 'I wonder if the Allisons will help us again?'

'But, Jim, what does the whole thing *mean*?'

Jim was turning over the pages of the telephone directory. .

'I don't know,' he said. 'Marjorie said emphatically that the police were not to know. But I'm not even sure that we'll be wise to keep it to ourselves.'

'What did she say?' demanded Angela.

Jim was giving the Allison's number and trying to think about Marjorie's conversation. She had said little, but had hinted at a great deal. The truth, as he understood it, was that unless he obeyed the instructions, Tub would be in danger. So if the police learned of their trip, Tub might suffer. Logic told him that it would be absurd to go to Canport without telling the police, but if Tub did come to any harm...

'Hallo. Is that Mr. Allison?'

'Yes.' Allison's voice was pleasant.

'This is Gantry here. I wonder if it's possible for you to drive us about twenty-five miles out of town tonight?'

'What's that?' asked Allison, startled.

'I know it sounds mad,' Jim said, 'but we've got to get to a

160

place twenty-five miles out of Malling, and——'

'Just a minute,' said Allison. 'Is this about your youngster? My wife's been telling me what happened.'

'It's about him, yes.'

'Then when do we start?' asked Allison calmly.

Jim said: 'If my wife and I leave here at once, and walk towards Malling, will you pick us up?'

'Yes, we'll do that,' promised Allison. 'I hope the news is good.'

'Fairly good,' said Jim. 'I don't know how to say thank you.'

'Oh, forget it,' said Allison gently.

He rang off. Jim put down the receiver.

'Now we've got to decide something about George.'

'He might take *ages* to wake up.'

'Yes,' said Jim, 'but——'

There was a movement on the landing and George appeared. That settled it. Jim told him to get his coat and that he would explain on the way. Then he poked his head into the kitchen.

'Paddy, if the police call and want to know where we've gone, tell them I shall try to ring them from Canham later on.'

'So it's to Canham you're going,' said Paddy sourly. ' 'Tis a crazy thing ye're doing, going out like this without telling a soul where ye might be. It's crazy, I tell ye, you shouldn't be doing it.'

'We've got to go,' said Jim.

' 'Tis madness,' said Paddy, obstinately, 'I'm not sure that I'll let ye go if ye don't take me wid ye.'

Angela was coming down the stairs.

'Paddy,' she said, 'if we don't do what we were told to do, Tub might get hurt.'

That silenced him, but he stood by the open front door watching them as they hurried down the drive. A policeman was standing on the lawn.

George said: 'They'll follow us, I expect.'

'We're being picked up in a few minutes,' said Jim, 'we shall be all right. We'd better leave explanations for a few minutes, George, but you must know this: we had a telephone call from Marjorie. She's all right, and she says Tub is safe.'

Jim did not know how much might depend on the success of their mission; he only knew that he could do nothing other than what he was doing.

They hurried towards the main road, crossed over and watched the headlights of several cars which were coming towards them.

A car slowed down. Allison was sitting next to his wife, who was driving. He leaned forward and opened the door, greeting them with a brisk: 'In you get.' As soon as the door had closed, Mrs. Allison turned the car and started back towards Malling. Not until they were clear of the street lights did any of them relax. Then Allison turned round in his seat, and said quietly:

'Where are we going?'

'Canport,' said Jim, and launched into the whole story. 'I don't know what to make of it,' he finished, 'except that *if* I'm right, they're using Tub to—to blackmail us into making this journey.'

'Obviously they are,' said Allison. 'Did Mrs. Langford say that he was with her?'

'No. Only that he was all right.'

'I suppose we are doing the right thing,' Angela said, in a small voice.

'I've been wondering whether we oughtn't to tell the police something,' Allison said. 'It's up to you, of course, but it might be a good idea, don't you think?'

Jim said: 'I want to, in one way, but if I tell them they'll get in touch with the Canport police, and the Red Lion will be watched. These people will probably know if the police are about. If we break faith, and they've got Tub——'

'Then we'd better not say anything,' Allison agreed.

'I've got an idea that might help,' said his wife, slowly. She was quiet for a moment, then went on briskly: 'Supposing we slow down on the outskirts of Canport, Mike, and you get out there. You can telephone the local police, or else Folly, and tell him what's happened. That would mean that the police will be able to take any action they think necessary, but not until after Mr. and Mrs. Gantry have got to the Red Lion.'

'What do you think, Gantry?' asked her husband.

'Yes, I think that covers it,' said Jim. 'I don't know where we should be if it weren't for you two people.'

'Oh, nonsense!' said Allison, gruffly.

'There's one thing I don't think you've considered,' said George.

His voice startled them. He had been sitting so quietly that Jim had almost forgotten that he was there.

He went on slowly: 'Lecky might not have been telling the truth. I've been thinking about this afternoon's affair. We took his word for it that Porton was concerned, but we certainly haven't any proof. We *do* know that the dark-haired fellow was there, but we don't know that the man has anything to do with Porton.'

'You're right about that, of course,' said Jim, 'but what point would there be in Lecky lying to us?'

George said: 'One very strong point.'

'I can't see it,' admitted Jim.

'Well, supposing Lecky was holding something back,' said George. 'He would talk about Porton or anyone, so as to put us off the scent, wouldn't he? It's the kind of thing which Lecky would do.'

'But we'd all assumed that Lecky was killed because he had followed Porton!' objected Jim.

'All we know is that he followed the dark-haired man,' George pointed out. 'I still think Porton might be a red-herring.'

'It doesn't make all that difference,' Allison said, cheerfully. 'You'll know more about it when you get to the Red Lion. The main thing is to get Tub back.'

No one made any further comment.

Suddenly, Allison said: 'I think we're being followed.'

Jim looked cautiously through the back window. The head-lights of a car were not far behind them.

George said: 'It came out of a side road, didn't it?'

'Yes, a couple of miles back.'

'Well, it might be anyone,' observed Jim.

'I noticed a car parked just off the main road, without lights,' Allison remarked, 'and a car came after us immediately afterwards. It might be a police car.'

'They *could* have telephoned here, I suppose,' said Mrs.

Allison, a little nervously. She was looking into the driving mirror. 'It's gaining on us.'

'Go faster!' cried Angela.

'We're doing nearly fifty,' said Allison.

They were, in fact, going much too fast for comfort.

Suddenly, they reached the crown of the hill. Five or six miles away, the lights of Canport glowed brightly. The road now ran downhill, and there were fewer twists and turns. They went faster, but once they were on the straight, the following car overhauled them without difficulty.

They sat tensely. The car behind drew close. Suddenly it pulled out, to pass them. Mrs. Allison jammed on the brakes.

'The ruddy fool!' exclaimed Allison.

'It's stopping!' cried Angela.

The big car pulled up in the middle of the road, so that there was no room on either side. Mrs. Allison was forced to stop.

Two or three men were already getting out of it.

'We must keep our heads,' said Allison. 'Gantry, you'd better be the spokesman. I'll have something to say to the police in the morning about the way they did that, but——'

'*They aren't policemen!*' whispered his wife.

One of the men looked in at the open door.

'Is Gantry there?'

'Yes,' said Jim.

'Get out,' said the man.

'Who——'

'Never mind who we are, get out. The rest of you turn back and take the first turning on the right. Wait there for Gantry. If he's a good boy, he'll be seeing you.' There was a mocking note in the man's voice.

Angela said: 'Jim, I'm coming with you!'

'You're not,' said the man in the doorway. He took Jim's arm. 'Come on, Gantry, we haven't time to waste.'

Allison said: 'Be damned to you!' He flung open his door, but a man was standing by it, and thrust him back. The man who had called to Jim snapped:

'Don't play the fool. We've got guns.'

There was a revolver in his hand. The effect of seeing its squat shape was the same on them all. They sat still.

164

Jim reached the road.

'Now, scram!' said the spokesman to the others. 'First on the right, don't forget. And don't play any tricks, or you won't see the kid again.'

Mrs. Allison put the engine into reverse. There was a field gate a little way behind her, and she turned the car there, then drove off. She had no choice, but as Jim watched the car disappearing, he shivered.

The man by his side said: 'Feeling cold, Gantry?'

Jim did not answer.

'Go and get in,' the man ordered.

Jim obeyed. The big car's engine was still switched on. He climbed into the back. The man with the gun sat on one side, a second man on the other. The doors closed, and the car moved off. It did not keep to the main road for long, but turned off about three miles outside Canport. The road it took was winding and narrow, but the driver went at speed. Soon, the headlights shone on a house, half-hidden by trees. The driver went straight through the open gates and pulled up.

'Get out.'

Jim obeyed, very conscious of the gun which was pointing towards him. His thoughts were in confusion. Why had they done this thing? Were these the people whom he had expected to meet at the Red Lion?

The house door opened.

'Inside,' said the spokesman, pushing Jim roughly before him. Once in the hall the man turned and looked at Jim. 'Did you tell the police about meeting someone at the Red Lion?'

'No.'

It all seemed so pointless; but there was an atmosphere here which frightened him. He stood looking at the spokesman and his two companions. There was nothing noteworthy about any of them—unless it was the fact that their caps were pulled low over their eyes.

The gunman motioned to the stairs.

'Go on up,' he said.

Jim obeyed, the three men following. There was a dim light on the landing. The only sound was that of their footsteps, muffled by the carpet.

'The room on the right.'

165

Jim opened the door and went in. The room was in darkness. He took another step forward, and then heard a movement behind him. He turned abruptly, but was too late to prevent the door from closing.

He stood for a moment in pitch darkness, his heart beating uncontrollably. Gradually, it steadied. He turned and groped for a light switch near the door. He found one, and pressed it down. A dim blue light came on, over a dressing-table. The room was a small one, with a single bed . . .

Tub was lying on the bed, asleep.

CHAPTER NINETEEN

TUB

With difficulty Jim restrained himself from rushing across the room and picking the child up. He could see that Tub was breathing evenly.

'*Oh, Tub!*' murmured Jim, bending over him. For a moment he forgot the men outside, forgot everything but the fact that Tub was safe. Then alarm surged through him. *Was* Tub asleep? He was lying so still, almost too still—but he *was* breathing. Very gently Jim lifted his hand; still Tub did not stir.

They had drugged him . . .

He tried to calm himself. There was no indication that Tub had been ill-treated. Probably he had been given a sedative, to make sure that he slept soundly. That was the most likely explanation. No one could injure a child . . .

He was so absorbed that he did not notice the door open. When Marjorie Langford said: 'Hello, Jim,' he spun round, stifling a cry.

'Tub's all right,' she told him, in a dull voice.

Her eyes, darkly circled, looked enormous in her tiny, heart-shaped face. Her cheeks were pale. All the events of that terrible day flashed through Jim's mind as he looked at her. He stepped forward and took her hand.

'You're looking tired,' he said.

'I've a terrible headache,' Marjorie told him. 'It keeps throbbing, it seems split in two.' She sank into a chair. 'Where are the others, Jim?'

'Somewhere along the road. They were told where to wait.'

'Jim, I—I wish it were possible to explain what has happened, but it isn't possible. I mustn't talk, it won't be safe for me to talk. I can tell you this. These men are *merciless*.'

'Who are they?' That 'merciless' was echoing in Jim's ears. She meant exactly what she said.

'I can't tell you. I don't know, Jim, and I'm not allowed to explain what's happened to me today. They've given me a few minutes with you, to tell you this: they mean all that they say. Don't take any chances with them. Don't defy them.'

'What are they going to say?'

'I don't know,' said Marjorie. 'They've used me as a go-between, that's all, and I daren't——'

'That's enough,' a man said.

Jim had not heard him come in. Now he stepped forward. He was a fatter man than any of the others. A scarf hid his features. And there was something fantastic about his appearance; his voice also was pitched on a high, unnatural key—an assumed voice, Jim felt sure.

'Come with me, Gantry,' the man ordered.

He led the way into a small study. It was pleasantly enough furnished. The man sat down and pointed to a chair.

'Mrs. Langford was right,' he said. 'I mean what I say. And I hold the child.' His voice was ominous.

Jim nodded.

'I hope that means you're going to be sensible. Now listen to me. Your wife went to the Dales' house the other night, and took some papers away. I'm going to have those papers, Gantry. I don't suppose you've got them with you——' He paused.

Jim kept silent.

'Have you or haven't you?' snapped the man.

Jim said mechanically: 'No, I haven't.'

The answer crystallised a thought which had flashed into his mind. It was taken for an admission that he *had* the mysterious papers. Well, if the other believed he had them, *they were a bargaining weapon*. By pretending that he had them his position would be stronger. For the first time since the hold-up, he saw a gleam of hope.

'All right, they're not here,' said the man. 'So you'll send your wife back to get them. She won't bring them here, she'll pass them over to my agent—I'll make arrangements for that to be done without the knowledge of the police. When I've got them you can have the child back. Is that clear?'

168

'Yes.'

'I'm going to send you back to the car you came in,' the man said, 'and you'll go and speak to your wife and tell her what to do.'

'There's one other thing,' said Jim.

He tried to make himself sound bold, but it was not easy. He drew in his breath.

'I'm taking my son back with me,' he said.

'Don't be a damned fool!'

'I've got the papers,' Jim said. 'You can have them *after* Tub's back at home, but not before.'

In the moment of silence that followed, he tried to assess his chances of success. Much depended on his coolness and show of confidence. If this man knew that his legs felt like water and his heart like a stone, there would be no chance of winning.

The man got up. Without speaking, he went out of the room. Cold sweat broke out on Jim's forehead. He heard heavy footsteps and a door opening. Marjorie cried out: 'No, don't!' There was an oath, and then the door closed again. The man returned. Jim steeled himself to look up.

Tub, still asleep, was in the man's arms. His head was lolling forward and it was now very evident that it was not a natural sleep.

Jim clenched his teeth.

The man sat down, with Tub on one knee, and said: 'I don't want to hurt the kid, Gantry, but you're going to do what you're told. Don't make any mistake about it. You're going to do what you're told.' He picked up the cigar and slowly lit it. 'You'll do as I say, or I'll press this on his forehead,' he said, 'and it will brand him for life.'

I mustn't be weak, Jim thought. God help me, I must see it through! He tried to avoid looking at Tub, but it was impossible. The child was so sound asleep, so sweet, so lovely.

'*Now* you see,' said the man, and held the cigar close to Tub's forehead.

Jim said quietly: 'If that touches him, you will never get the papers. It is also unlikely that you will get out of here alive.' He stood up.

'Sit down!'

Jim was aware, then, of another man in the room. He was

169

armed. It was the man who had brought Jim from the main road. He was looking at his leader who was staring furiously at Jim.

Jim leaned forward and in a wild sweep wrest the child from the man's arms.

'Now I'll go and give the message to my wife,' he cried.

'*Put him down!*'

'You either want the papers or you don't,' said Jim. 'I've told you the conditions on which you can have them. It's up to you.'

The man was no longer sure of himself.

The armed guard stood expectantly, but no orders were given. The room was very still. Jim did not move. He was trying to imagine what might follow. Marjorie was still here; he ought to make some effort to get her away. What chance had she got, with men like this?

The man leaned forward.

'I'm not taking *any* chances, Gantry,' he said. 'You'll either do as you're told, or I'll have your house searched and get those papers.'

Jim said: 'The police are watching the house too closely. You haven't any more chance of searching it now than you had before.'

'I can handle the police!'

'You haven't made a very good job of it so far,' said Jim. 'Well, what's it to be?'

Out of the corner of his eye Jim saw the gun move. Anything might happen now. He held his breath.

There was a shout of alarm downstairs.

It came without any warning, a single cry followed by a thud and a scuffle. Jim swung round towards the door, but as he did so the window crashed in and the curtains billowed into the room. The man with the gun cried out, the man at the desk jumped to his feet.

Then Cunningham sprang from the window into the room.

It all happened so quickly that Jim did not see the significance of that, but he did see the gunman pointing his weapon at Cunningham. Jim kicked out. He caught the man on the leg, and spoiled his aim. The roar of a shot crashed out. Other policemen swarmed in behind Cunningham, and the kidnappers turned and ran.

The sounds of wild scuffling came from downstairs.

Shouts, thuds and the banging of doors followed. Jim stood quite still, his heart beating so fast that he felt suffocated. He staggered to a chair and sat down, Tub in his arms. It was over, that terrible strain had passed, the police were in possession and Tub was safe. It did not matter to him whether the men were caught, nothing mattered but Tub.

He closed his eyes, but hardly had he done so when the telephone rang.

At first, he regarded it only as an additional noise to the din that filled the house, but it kept ringing. He leaned forward and lifted the receiver.

'Hallo.'

'Porton——' a man said.

'Hallo, who is that?' asked Jim.

The voice came again, but it was now indistinct and doubtful. 'Is that Porton?'

'Speaking,' said Jim.

So Porton was concerned.

The man at the other end rang off.

Jim began to take more interest in what was going on in the house. In the din and hullabaloo that was coming from downstairs, he thought he recognised Folly's voice. He went to the door, and saw both him and Cunningham coming up the stairs. Then he thought of Marjorie. The door of her room was closed.

Folly said: 'Well, Gantry?'

At any other time, Jim would have sensed that there was something on the Yard man's mind, that his voice held an ominous ring. Now, all he thought about was Marjorie. She might be hurt. He hurried across the landing, and tried the handle. The door was locked.

Folly and Cunningham joined him.

'Mrs. Langford should be in there!'

Folly did not hesitate. He tried the handle and, when he found the door locked, put his shoulder to it. It resisted his first efforts. Cunningham joined in the assault, and the door creaked, then gave way.

Folly went in first, Cunningham followed and Jim brought

171

up the rear.

He felt terribly afraid for Marjorie.

She had been in here, he had heard her protest when Porton had taken Tub away. Anything might have happened to her.

Folly and Cunningham moved forward to the bed. There Marjorie was lying, with a stocking tied round her neck, her eyes bulging, her tongue protruding from between her teeth,

There had been much activity after Marjorie had been discovered. Folly and Cunningham, ignoring Jim, telephoned for a doctor and gave Marjorie first aid. After a while, Folly had peremptorily ordered Jim out of the room. This time, Jim put the Superintendent's manner down to the shock of finding Marjorie, and thought little of it. He went back to the study. A policeman on the landing followed him. Jim sat down, and looked up with a weary smile.

There was hostility in the answering glance.

A little surprised, but putting it down as a natural surliness, Jim got up and went to the door.

'Stay where you are, please.'

There was no doubt now of the man's unamiability. Jim's disquiet increased. He heard a car draw up outside, and footsteps in the hall and on the stairs and, clearly, a man's voice on the landing. Then a door closed.

Jim began to worry about Marjorie. The sight of her face was constantly in his mind's eye. He had never seen anyone look quite so ghastly.

He had not heard a car leave the house, nor had he heard much sounds of activity outside. The indications were that Porton and the other men in the house had all been captured and were now in one of the downstairs rooms. The affair was practically over. True, there was the man who had telephoned Porton; the police ought to be told about him.

How had they come to find the house?

Then the door opened, and Folly came in. The man's face was stony, uncompromising. What on earth had happened to him?

Folly said: 'Now you'll tell me where those papers are, Gantry.'

CHAPTER TWENTY

SUSPICION

'*Papers?*' Jim said. He spoke blankly, startled by the question.

Folly snapped: 'The truth please. You admitted to Porton that you have the papers. Where are they?'

'But I've never had any papers!'

Folly looked at him coldly, furiously. It was difficult to believe that such a comfortable collection of ripples and pink chins could look so ferocious. 'Don't lie to me!'

Jim restrained himself with difficulty.

'I told Porton that I had some papers because it was the only weapon I had to use against him. I suppose Cunningham heard us talking.'

'He did.'

'Then he must have heard what the man intended to do.'

'He heard everything,' said Folly, ominously, 'including your admissions and your attempt to bargain with Porton. Your wife went to Mrs. Dale's house and brought something away, and I want to know what she brought away and where I shall find it. Is that understood?'

Jim said: 'I bluffed Porton too well, apparently.'

'You will not bluff me,' retorted Folly.

'It seems that I have done so.' Jim shrugged his shoulders. 'How is Mrs. Langford?'

'You're very interested in her, aren't you?'

'Of course I am.'

'Although you insisted that you hardly knew her until she came to stay at your house,' said Folly. He made an impatient gesture. 'You'd better come with me.'

The absurd business went on. Under guard, Jim was taken downstairs. A blanket was brought for Tub, and Jim carried the child into a police car. There were several cars there now. In one of them were the men who had been at the house earlier. They were morose and helpless, with a police driver in front. The fat man glared at Jim. Porton, thought Jim. At least he knows that I'm not involved. Surely he'll talk!

A policeman got in beside him. Folly took the wheel. Cunningham, apparently, was going to stay at the house. There was no sign of Marjorie, but as Folly drove out of the drive, an ambulance drew up.

Soon they were speeding rather erratically along the road. Heaven help us! Jim thought as for the third time they narrowly missed a telegraph pole. Folly may be a good sleuth but he's certainly a hell of a driver. Cunningham knew what he was about when he stayed behind!

He said quietly: 'Do you know where my wife is, Superintendent?'

'She has been taken into Malling,' Folly said shortly.

It was not wise to ask Folly too many questions. His pink hands were safer on the wheel than waving about in the air. Worried and anxious Jim kept silent.

Why had they sent Angela into Malling? Why had they not allowed her to come to Porton's house? The police must have known full well that she was desperately anxious to see Tub. They might be suspicious of him, but surely they did not suspect Angela?

He drew in a sharp breath. Of course they suspected her! She had probably been taken into Malling police station. If only the wild idea of going to see Mrs. Dale had never occurred to her; and if only he had discouraged it.

The car sped on.

At half-past one that morning, Colonel Maitland entered the office. He looked as fresh as if it were midday. Folly, whose eyes were red-rimmed, was stifling a yawn. He was alone, and the papers on the desk were in great disorder.

Maitland gave his twinkling smile.

'You're keeping late hours, Folly.'

'Too late, for my liking,' remarked Folly. For a moment he brightened. 'Would you like a cup of tea or chocolate?'

'Tea, please,' said Maitland, stretching his long legs. 'And

174

who's our man?'

'Porton, as the active agent,' Folly told him, 'and Gantry as the root of it.'

Maitland frowned. 'Are you sure of Gantry?'

Folly threw up his hands. 'All the indications are that it's Gantry, but I must admit I'm not *entirely* satisfied.'

'Doesn't Porton know?'

'That's one of the odd things about it,' said Folly, 'if Porton's telling the truth, and I think he is, because he wants to throw the blame for the murders on his employer, Porton *doesn't* know who he's been working for. I'd better tell you the story from the beginning, hadn't I?'

'I think it would be as well.'

Scrupulously exact, Folly went into details about what had happened that evening, and then, visibly brightening after a constable had brought in tea and sandwiches, he ran over his conclusions and the reasons for them.

'We have always thought that Mrs. Gantry's call on Mrs. Dale was important,' he said. 'Not only was there the attack on her, but also the fact that immediately afterwards the child was kidnapped. That suggested to me that the Gantrys had some papers, perhaps the will, which some other person wanted. By taking the child, the kidnapping was a powerful weapon to use against them.'

'Hmm,' said Maitland.

'I have also found it hard to believe that the Langfords and the Gantrys were comparative strangers,' went on Folly, 'and it seemed to me that the Langfords had the strongest possible motive to murder Coombs. Not necessarily both of them, but one or the other. The question was to decide which one. Both of them had the opportunity. Langford, in spite of the attacks which he appears to suffer, has strength enough. His wife, on the other hand, is a small woman whose physical strength might not have been enough to injure Coombs as badly as he was injured. Therefore, I concentrated on George Langford. If Coombs died, and there was no will, his wife could come into a fortune and he, naturally, would share it. One of the rocks on which his marriage has broken has been his lack of money.'

Maitland nodded.

'There, then, were the bare bones of the situation as I saw

it,' said Folly. 'The Gantrys themselves are not wealthy, and it seemed to me that if they discovered that Langford had killed Coombs, they might have helped him afterwards, thus becoming accessories after the fact, to get what he most wanted, the will. Once Langford had his hands on his wife's money, of course, he could have paid the Gantrys well for their help.

'There were two complications.

'First, the series of burglaries. In spite of all the evidence to the contrary, I have never been satisfied that O'Hara and the Gantrys were innocent of those. Porton's evidence was the most important factor on O'Hara's behalf. As Porton is now known to be involved, that evidence is worthless. In other words, the first lines along which Cunningham and Forrest were working appear to be the right ones.'

'I see,' murmured Maitland.

'So we can now set aside the burglary complication,' went on Folly. 'The second is the love affair between Marjorie Langford and Andrew Dale. It is quite clear that George Langford knew that Dale had won his wife's affections. Langford is the quiet, brooding type. It is not difficult to imagine him seeking revenge. What better revenge could he have than seeing Andrew Dale convicted of murdering his uncle? None, I think. There were undoubtedly indications that Dale had a motive, which would certainly have served Langford's purpose. I think things first began to go wrong when, after Coombs was murdered, his will was lost. An effort had to be made immediately either to find, or destroy it. I wondered whether Langford, hating Dale as he must do, had set fire to the building to secure two things—first, the destruction of the will, and second, the death of Dale. If he were able afterwards to provide evidence that Dale was guilty, Langford's troubles would have been over. Is that all clear, sir?'

'Perfectly,' said Maitland.

'Of course, Langford himself could not do all the things which were done,' Folly went on. 'He had to have outside help—and that help, undoubtedly, came from Porton. Now, I had to find a connection between Porton and Langford. There was only one I could see: through Gantry. If Gantry, Porton and O'Hara were all three concerned in the burglaries, then Porton would do, or arrange for his men to do, whatever else was necessary. One must assume that at some stage or other, Porton and Gantry fell out. I imagine Gantry wanted more than his share of the proceeds. Gantry, in any case, was obviously trying to clear O'Hara by setting us on Porton's trail, through the dark-haired fellow whom we've got now, and the other ginger-haired man. At no time did Porton *know* Gantry was the man through whom he worked these burglaries. Gantry kept in the background. But after Mrs. Gantry had visited Mrs. Dale and got the will, Porton guessed who Gantry was. The possession of the will, of course, was a powerful weapon in the hands of either Gantry or Porton. As long as either of them had it, Langford would always be in danger of blackmail. His wife would inherit the Coombs fortune, but either of the others could prove that she had no right to it. Langford would be in a very difficult position indeed.'

'I see,' said Maitland, pouring himself out another cup of tea.

'Now we get a little further along,' Folly said. 'Having guessed that the man who always worked in the dark was Gantry, Porton kidnapped the child. I ought to say here that I do not believe Mrs. Gantry knew anything of what was going on, although I have detained her for the moment. Gantry had to work very fast. He says that he had a telephone call from Mrs. Langford this evening, asking him to go to the Red Lion, Canport. He persuaded the Allisons to go with him. Luckily, our men watching the Gantry's house were on the alert, telephoned us from a nearby house, and enabled us to send a car to follow the Gantrys and the Allisons. Owen was responsible for that job, sir, and very well he did it.

'Now, there *appeared* to be a hold-up. But remember that the Allisons, neither of whom had any interest in the affair in spite of my earlier doubts about them, would be excellent witnesses to that hold-up. They would, in other words, testify that Gantry could not help himself in going to see Porton. But I think Gantry knew what was going to happen, chose that way to put himself in the clear and then went on to have a showdown with Porton. He denies even knowing that the man he talked to was Porton, but if the rest of his story is untrue, then that is untrue as well. There was some talk, and Porton threatened the child. Cunningham was actually outside the window.

177

He heard the conversation. He heard Gantry admit that he had these papers. Gantry now says that he was bluffing, in order to bargain for the safety of the child, but that hardly holds water.'

'I suppose not,' said Maitland.

'I don't see how it can,' said Folly. 'Anyhow, we ought to know soon. The Gantrys' house is being searched, and if anything is found we'll have our case.'

'I see,' said Maitland. 'Is there anything else?'

'Several other things, sir,' said Folly. 'Mrs. Langford, for instance—and this is one of the worst features of the affair—was nearly murdered. In fact it isn't certain that she will recover. I've put it about that we expect her to die without making a statement. That may make someone careless. Now if she automatically inherited after Coombs's death, on her death Langford would inherit. In my view, Gantry tried to kill her, so that she would not provide any further complications.'

Maitland said: 'You're making Gantry out a most cold-blooded devil, aren't you?'

'The murderer and the mind behind all this *is* cold-blooded,' declared Folly. 'I think that's what happened to Mrs. Langford. I'm hoping she will come round long enough to identify Gantry as her assailant.'

'You don't know how she came to be at Porton's house, do you?' asked Maitland.

'Yes. Porton has told me. He had instructions first to take the child and then to take Mrs. Langford to look after it. Porton thought that the unknown man had thus played into his hands, and gave instructions to his own men to carry out both kidnappings.'

'I don't quite follow Porton's part,' Maitland admitted.

'It's really very simple, sir. He has business interests up and down the country, some legal, many illegal. He's a receiver of stolen goods in a big way. He has admitted that. He says that the man whom he now believes was Gantry discovered some of his criminal activities and blackmailed him into giving assistance. I think that is a satisfactory explanation of Porton's part, don't you?'

'But there's still doubt about Gantry,' Maitland pointed out.

'A little,' admitted Folly. 'I'm hoping to hear from his

house at any time.'

'Meanwhile, you've got the Gantrys here?'

'Yes.'

'What about the Allisons?'

'They've gone home. I've a man watching them.'

'George Langford?'

'He's at Canport Hospital, by his wife's side. And we've someone with her, too.'

'You haven't charged Langford?'

'Not yet.'

'What about the Dales, mother and son?' asked Maitland.

'Andrew Dale knows nothing about the latest developments,' said Folly. 'I thought it wiser to get the case complete before he was told anything. His mother is at home. There isn't very much doubt about Mrs. Dale's part.'

'It puzzles me very much,' said Maitland.

'Well, sir, she has the reputation of being a stiff-necked and narrow-minded woman. To find her only son carrying on, as she would call it, with a married woman, would be something of a blow. Of course, she blames the woman, not her son. I think she has Coombs's will, for she and Coombs were good friends.'

'Why didn't she produce it when Coombs died?' asked Maitland.

'She kept it to bargain with Mrs. Langford, I suspect. I think she called to deliver an ultimatum to Mrs. Langford, that Gantry saw her, discovered what she was after, and told her that if she gave the will to his wife when she called later, he would make sure that Andrew and Marjorie broke off their *affair*.'

'Have you seen Mrs. Dale?'

'Not yet, sir. I want to leave the Dales to the last.'

'Well, it all *sounds* very convincing,' agreed Maitland. 'Have you found Mrs. Gantry's handbag?'

'Yes, at Porton's.'

'What about Lecky's murder?'

'Lecky always concentrated on the Gantrys,' said Folly. 'I think something he said at the Antelope in Canham warned Gantry that he had discovered the truth. Gantry had as good an opportunity as any of them to kill Lecky. And in that con-

179

nection,' went on Folly, 'there is something I forgot to tell you, sir, and it's of extreme importance. The dark-haired man did *not* kill Lecky. It must have been one of those at the Antelope.'

'Can you prove it?'

'Conclusively, sir. The dark-haired man tried to interfere with the Allisons' car, to make sure that Porton had time to get away. Porton had been at the George, as Lecky discovered, presumably giving orders to his men. The dark-haired man dashed off by a back way and caught a bus. He says it was passing through the town and he jumped on it. While making inquiries in Canham, we did have evidence that a man boarded a moving bus, which left Canham dead on schedule. Lecky was alive at the time the bus passed through the village. There are several witnesses to that.'

'I *see*,' said Maitland, heavily. 'What about the second burglary at the Gantrys' house?'

'Porton's man,' said Folly. 'Porton tells me that he already suspected Gantry and was trying to get proof. That covers only the second burglary. Porton was responsible for the first, too. He wanted to get what he could from the Langfords' luggage and if, as I think, he wanted something to use as blackmail, that's a straightforward explanation.' Folly smiled. 'It cuts out my earlier suspicion that the Gantrys staged those burglaries from the inside, but we can't expect to have everything, can we?'

'I suppose not,' said Maitland. 'Have you got a statement from Porton?'

'He's writing it now, sir.'

'And the Gantrys refuse to admit anything?'

The telephone bell rang, and Folly moved his hand out for it at once.

'Hallo,' he said, 'Folly speaking.' He glanced at Maitland, his small eyes twinkling with excitement. 'Yes, from Gantry's house, go on ... You're sure?' He listened with obvious satisfaction, and then added: 'Bring it here at once.' Then he replaced the receiver and looked triumphantly at Maitland. 'The will was in Gantry's study, behind a bookcase. I think that's *that*, sir.'

CHAPTER TWENTY-ONE

FINAL BLOW

Twenty minutes later, when the will was brought into the office, Maitland and Folly pored over it. The legal phraseology was difficult to follow, and both were tired, but it was not long before they established one fact: old Coombs had disinherited Marjorie Langford.

Maitland said: 'Then who gets his money?'

Folly ran his finger down the typewritten lines.

'Dale gets five thousand pounds and his mother gets another five. Mere chicken-feed. The rest goes to charities. That means that the only people who could suffer from this will are the Langfords!'

'Then you've your case against Langford,' said Maitland. 'All you have to establish is the Gantrys' complicity, and it's over. You'll see Mrs. Dale now, won't you?'

'Yes, sir. She won't like being woken up at this hour, but she's more likely to be shocked into telling the truth. I think I'll go along, without giving her warning.'

'I should,' agreed Maitland. He stood up. 'There's one other thing, Folly. The attempt to poison Langford—if it *was* an attempt to do so.'

Folly laughed.

'I think I can explain that, sir! Dr. Lawson discovered that for his everyday treatment Langford was given powders, in which was a small amount of strychnine. If someone had substituted a stronger powder, that would account for the attacks. It could have been done by Langford himself, or by Gantry, who admitted to me that he knew Langford took these powders, but was very vague about them.'

'But surely Gantry wanted him to keep alive?'

'The dose wasn't enough to kill him,' Folly pointed out. 'If

181

self-administered, it would scare Gantry into thinking that Langford was going to kill himself. If Gantry gave it to him, it would be a sharp reminder to Langford that he had better do as he was told, or he would know what was coming to him.'

'I see,' said Maitland, slowly.

Folly got into his car and drove to the Dales' house. Marlborough Avenue was almost in darkness, for the street lamps had been turned low. There were no lights in any of the windows. After slightly grazing the gate-post, Folly pulled up outside the house. He was very tired. Pulling himself together he walked to the front door.

After three long rings of the bell, a bolt was drawn back and Andrew Dale opened the door.

'Who is it? Oh, Folly!' Andrew backed away in surprise. 'You'd better come in.' He led the way into the drawing-room. 'Well, what can I do for you?'

'I really want a word with your mother,' said Folly.

'My dear chap, have a heart! You can't disturb her at this time of night.'

'I'm afraid I must,' said Folly.

'There's no "must" about it,' said Andrew testily. 'The rule is that police interrogations should be carried out by two officers, you know that as well as I do.'

Folly said slowly: 'You're not being very helpful, Mr. Dale.'

'There are limits to helpfulness,' said Andrew. 'Send for someone else, if you feel you really must wake my mother up. I think it's going too far, but presumably you know your business.'

'I do. May I use the telephone?'

As he telephoned, Folly reflected that Dale had scored a point; he should not have come alone. Nor would he have done so, had he not been so tired. It would take another man a quarter of an hour to get here. He gave the instructions over the telephone, and then sat back in an easy chair. Andrew offered him a drink.

Folly declined.

'Well I think I'll go and put a few clothes on,' said Andrew. 'It looks like being a long session.'

When he returned, fully dressed, they sat there, exchanging

182

occasional words, until another car drew up outside. Andrew let the detective-officer in, then led the way upstairs into his mother's room.

Andrew touched her forehead. 'Mother, wake up.'

She opened her eyes. Andrew smiled down at her.

'It's all right,' he said, 'there are two gentlemen to see you, that's all—they've one or two questions to ask.' Andrew arranged the pillows behind her, and helped her to sit up. 'Now take your time, mother, there's nothing to worry about.'

'Who *are* these men?'

'I am a police officer, Mrs. Dale,' said Folly.

'A police officer! But this is outrageous! What do you mean by coming into my bedroom? Andrew! What are you thinking of to allow such a thing as this to happen? I insist—I *insist* that you leave at once.'

'Mother——' began Andrew.

'I won't talk to them!' cried Mrs. Dale. 'It's an outrage, absolutely an outrage!'

'If it will suit you better, I will wait outside until you get up,' Folly said.

'I won't talk to you! I've nothing to say to you!'

'Mother, please——' began Andrew.

'Be quiet! *You* ought to know better!' She glared from one man to the other, and then drew in her breath. Folly thought that she looked frightened. 'I won't——'

'I needn't keep you long,' Folly said, gently. 'Why did you go to see Mrs. Gantry the other night, Mrs. Dale, and what did you give her when she came here?'

'I didn't go to see her, I went to see Mrs. Langford!' Her voice was shrill, she looked wildly about her, almost as if she were trying to find some way of escape. 'Go away! I won't talk to you, I won't——'

Andrew put his hand on her shoulder. He looked grave, and his voice was compelling.

'Mother, you mustn't behave like this. *Did* you give Mrs. Gantry anything?'

'No, no, no! Andrew, order them out of the house!'

'You must calm yourself,' Andrew insisted. 'You'll make them think that you did give Mrs. Gantry something.'

His mother stiffened, stared at him—and then collapsed.

183

She began to cry, while the police stood uncomfortably and Andrew tried to soothe her.

Then the door opened, and a middle-aged woman in a flannel dressing-gown came in. She hurried across the room, but before she reached the bed, Andrew looked up.

'Go downstairs and make a cup of tea, Maude, will you?'

'But the mistress——'

'I'll look after her.'

The woman hesitated, but went out. The older woman's cries became more subdued. Folly, watching, became convinced that there was something behind this passionate outburst, and that he would soon get what he wanted.

'I know I shouldn't have done it, Andrew,' she murmured, 'but I did it for your sake. I was thinking only of you.'

'But what *did* you do?'

'I—I gave her the will!' cried Mrs. Dale. 'She said she would make that Jezebel stop hanging around you if I gave it to her. Arnold entrusted it to me, he was afraid that someone was going to murder him, he gave it to me, and I——'

Andrew looked bleakly at Folly.

'Is that what you want?' he demanded.

'We needn't worry you any more,' said Folly.

'So you're after the Gantrys again,' Andrew said, bitterly. 'If I hadn't heard her myself, I should never have believed it.' He smoothed down his hair. 'I'd like to come along and see the Gantrys. I want to offer them my services.'

'I've no objection to that, of course,' said Folly stiffly.

Jim sat in a small room that was half-cell, half-bed-sitting-room, staring into space. Somewhere in this building Angela was with Tub: he did not know for certain whether she, like himself, was under arrest.

At least he had been allowed a few minutes with her, and knew that Tub was all right. How long ago it seemed since they had been together at their house, with no thought of danger or threat of trouble. Surely it was impossible for the police to prove him guilty of a crime he had not committed?

He had heard the police talking, and gathered that they suspected him, too, of the attack on Marjorie. It was so ridiculous that it was almost laughable, but they *meant* it.

Someone had attacked Marjorie.

Someone had killed Lecky. He had not realised how much the newspaperman had meant to him until he had gone. He wished he could see him now, with his broad grin and untidy clothes and his air of confidence. Lecky had been convinced that he knew who had killed Coombs and who had kidnapped Tub. Well, he had not been far wrong in naming Porton, but obviously there was someone besides Porton. The man who had telephoned him at Porton's house was probably guilty, but how could he find out who the man was?

He had not yet told Folly about that telephone call. Folly had made him so angry that he had forgotten all about it. To think he had strangled Marjorie——

Was she alive?

He looked at his watch. It was nearly three o'clock. He got up and walked about the room, peering along the passage. The door at the end of it opened, and two or three men appeared. He heard Andrew's voice, then Folly's. Andrew came hurrying along the passage, and the policeman opened the door.

'Jim, I'm terribly sorry about this.'

'Not half as sorry as I am,' said Jim, trying to laugh.

Andrew said: 'Jim, I know my way about in legal affairs. I hope you'll be guided by me.'

'Of course I will.'

'Then tell the whole truth,' said Andrew, bluntly. 'My mother has told Folly that she gave Angela the will. I don't see how we can get past that. Your *only* chance is to make it clear that you were acting under coercion, forced by George to do what you did.' He paused, as Jim stared at him in amazement. 'I'm serious,' Andrew insisted. 'I haven't got long, so we mustn't waste time. It's clear to me that there were threats against Tub and that you had to do what you were told, but you won't help yourself by general denials. The evidence is too damning.'

Jim said: 'Your mother told Folly that *Angela* had the will? What utter nonsense!'

'It isn't,' insisted Andrew. 'I gather from a remark of the Chief Constable's that they found the will at your house. I tell you the evidence is too strong. Your only chance is to justify yourself, and the jury will consider threats against Tub a sufficient justification. I've no doubt that George killed Coombs and, later, killed Lecky, but unless you make it clear that he was working on you, *you* may be blamed for that.' He lowered his voice. 'It seems that Marjorie is dying without having made a statement. Someone murdered *her*, remember.'

Jim said slowly: 'Are you telling me that you really believe I am implicated?'

Andrew looked at him oddly. 'Well, what else can I do? The evidence is undeniable, Jim. You must be reasonable. And after all, my mother isn't a liar. She was misguided, she shouldn't have conceded the will or interfered, but there it is.'

Jim stood back. 'Listen to me,' he said. 'Your mother did not give Angela the will. Neither Angela nor I knew that the will was at our house, and I'm not sure that it was found there. I did not conspire with George. He did not exert any pressure of any kind on me. Is that clear?' He had difficulty in keeping his voice steady.

Andrew looked grave. 'I can't do more than advise you, Jim. I know you'll be wise to accept my advice, but whether you do or not is entirely up to you.'

'I think you'd better go,' said Jim.

'Jim, be reasonable. I——'

'Oh, get out!'

Andrew shrugged his shoulders.

'I wish you wouldn't take this attitude,' he said, slowly. 'I would like to help you all I can, but there are limits to what I can do. If you conceal the truth, you'll help no one, and only damn yourself. That's the position, Jim. Porton has told all he knows.'

Jim said nothing, and Andrew turned away.

As he turned, the name Porton echoed in Jim's mind. He was back in the room at Porton's house, the din was all about him, the telephone bell added to it. He lifted the receiver and he heard the name: 'Porton,' and then a pause. When the man spoke again it was in a muffled voice which he could not recognise, but suddenly he knew that it was Andrew who had made that call, Andrew's voice had said: 'Porton?' just as he had said it now.

He saw, in a flash, how this affair had been turned against

186

him, how from the first Andrew had worked against George Langford, hating him because of Marjorie. He saw how the case had developed, with Paddy being suspected, being a ready-made suspect. He was sure that Andrew had persuaded his mother to give false evidence; he was sure that Andrew had hidden the will where it would be found and used as evidence that he had conspired with George.

Folly came up as Andrew opened the door.

'There's nothing I can do,' said Andrew.

Careful, thought Jim, careful. If I say the wrong thing, I'm finished.

Folly was looking at him, bleakly.

It would be impossible to prove anything now, but it was just possible to switch suspicion to Andrew, to make Folly take up a new line of investigation.

'Oh, Andrew,' he said, in a friendly voice.

Andrew turned, as if eagerly.

'It looks as if I shall have to do something,' Jim said. 'We'll see. What was the telephone number of Porton's house near Canport, do you know?'

'Hillsea 59,' said Andrew, just as quickly and simply as that.

Jim's voice changed. 'And how did you know that?'

Andrew started. 'Look here——'

Jim said: 'Folly, will you find out who telephoned Porton's house at Hillsea tonight, just after you arrived? I think you'll find that Dale made that call. Try, won't you?'

Andrew turned on his heel, but the colour had drained from his cheeks.

'And I don't think Mrs. Dale will stand up to cross-examination,' Jim went on. 'She would do anything for you, Andrew, but a good counsel will make hay of her evidence.'

He felt absurdly light-hearted, for Folly was looking oddly at Andrew, who stood, bereft of words.

CHAPTER TWENTY-TWO

LETTER FROM LECKY

Folly managed to get a few hours' sleep before he went to the office next morning. He arrived soon after nine o'clock.

After the interview in the police cell, Dale's manner had worried him, but he could not get in touch with the Malling operator who had been on duty at the time of the call to Hillsea 59, which Gantry had talked about. He had discovered from Hillsea that there had been such a call, of short duration. After that, there had been nothing he could do until morning.

If Dale had sent that call, it meant a complete change of tactics. His first job must be to check it.

Cunningham, looking washed out, was in the office.

'Hallo,' said Folly. 'How did you get on at Hillsea?'

'I found nothing, except evidence that Porton has been a fence for years, and that we can get him on twenty counts,' said Cunningham. 'There's nothing fresh on the Gantrys at all. Haven't we got enough evidence against him?'

'Not yet,' said Folly. 'That is——' He broke off, seeing a letter propped up on the desk, addressed to him. 'That's Lecky's writing,' he declared.

Cunningham looked startled. '*Lecky?* It arrived by the first post.'

'He must have posted it just before he left for Canham,' said Cunningham, looking at the postmark. 'He didn't, though —he posted it in Canham!' He watched Folly opening it, with growing excitement. 'Why should he do that?'

'He might have known that he was in danger,' said Folly. He smoothed out the letter, and then read quickly. As his eye travelled down the page his expression altered. Seeing it, unable to wait in patience, Cunningham cried agonisingly:

'What is it?'

Folly said grimly: 'Let this be a lesson to me!' He placed the letter firmly in front of his colleague. 'Well, this fixes Dale.'

'*Dale!*' exclaimed Cunningham, and then turned to the letter. 'Good lord!' He began to read aloud:

... I wonder, Folly, if you have seen one motive which would explain the mystery. If *Dale* is the murderer, everything, I think, would be explained very simply. Supposing Dale has been embezzling his clients' money? Coombs would get to know, and have to be silenced. The records would have to be destroyed, as they were destroyed in the fire. (By the way, Dale might easily have waited a few minutes too long before getting away. He would want to make it look as if he were in danger, wouldn't he?) The will would have to be lost, too, so that Marjorie Langford would inherit. Dale, I feel sure, expects to get rid of Langford and marry Marjorie. That would solve all his problems. I think him capable of trying to get Langford convicted of the murder. I think he's working on the Gantrys', too, as a second line of defence. Watch him.

One thing I do know. Dale has a hold over Porton, who is a complete scoundrel. I overheard Dale telephoning Porton and telling him what to do about the child—to use all possible pressure against the Gantrys. I think Dale has an idea that I suspect him, and he might try to deal with me as he did with old Coombs. So if this letter is my valediction—but I'm getting morbid!—I'll be seeing you!

Cunningham stopped reading, and looked blankly at Folly, who said slowly:

'He got there, all right. And Dale nearly got away with it. I'll get to work on Mrs. Dale.' He laughed, bitterly. 'Dale put her up to the story last night, he went to see her when he told me he was getting some clothes on. The man fooled me completely.' Folly's voice swelled with magnanimity, with humility.

'Can we get him?' demanded Cunningham.

189

'It won't be easy, but I think so. Much depends on Mrs. Langford. Has she come round?'

'She's improving,' Cunningham said.

'When Dale was talking to Gantry last night, he made it clear that he thought she would die. That probably made him over confident. I——'

The telephone bell rang.

'I'll get along,' said Folly. 'If it's Maitland, tell him I'll ring him later.' He went to the door, but Cunningham suddenly shouted:

'Wait a moment! Mrs. Langford's come round, and she's talked!' He whipped out a pencil. 'Yes, I'm ready ... She was acting under compulsion—Dale's compulsion ... He told her that he had evidence that would hang her husband ... Yes, yes, go on ... She was attracted by Dale but soon found out that she loved Langford ... Thought Langford was up to no good ... Fooled him, in the hope of learning the truth ... Dale had the child kidnapped, she was taken to a quiet side street where the child was waiting in a car ... Yes, go on,' Cunningham said into the telephone. 'Yes ... She was wanted to look after the child, as soon as the police arrived at Porton's house one of the men attacked her. Which one ... Pity. Is that all?'

He rang off, and stood staring at Folly.

'Well, that's that,' he said.

The Gantrys got out of their taxi in front of the house. Paddy was on the drive, and held his arms out to Tub, who seemed to regard the whole affair as a great joke.

They now knew the whole story of how Lecky had hit on the truth and, almost as if he had a premonition of his own fate, had written to Folly.

It all started by Andrew's defalcations, and its discovery by old Coombs. In an attempt to replace what he had embezzled, Andrew had blackmailed Porton. Then he had seen the likeness between Paddy and the real thief, one of Porton's tic-tac men, and played upon that likeness. He had lived hour by hour, first persuading George and Marjorie to go to Bligh Avenue, simply to get them out of his house, then seeing how that could be turned to advantage, and suspicion turned towards his friends.

The police had discovered, too, that Andrew had obtained a supply of strychnine, through a chemist acquaintance of Porton's, and poisoned George—and they remembered that just prior to each of George's seizures, Andrew had been left alone, for long enough to slip strychnine into a dose of George's medicine. And it was Andrew who had planted the will on them . . .

It was almost too much to learn that George's London doctor had told Folly that there was no reason why George should not fully recover. George and Marjorie faced an assured future, for George would be able to work again.

'Thank heavens it's over, my sweet,' Jim said. 'I would never have thought any man capable of such devilry, least of all Andrew. The police have even unearthed someone who saw Andrew taking a can of petrol into the office on the night of the fire.'

'Don't let's talk about it,' Angela said quickly. 'Oh, Paddy, I'm so hungry. What can you find for lunch?'

'Sure and there's plenty in the larder,' said Paddy. 'It's a cold lunch ye'll be wanting, and never did I get one ready with a lighter heart, so I'm telling ye. Tub! Come with Paddy, and I'll see what I can find ye.'

Waiting for lunch Jim remembered Lecky panting beside him on the stairs. He seemed to hear Lecky's voice and see his round, cheerful face. If Lecky had been less mysterious, he might be alive today.

Suddenly, he hurried into the hall, took up the telephone, and asked for Folly.

'Hallo, Folly,' he said. 'It's Gantry here. I've been wondering if you'll send a copy of Lecky's letter to *The Record*. It would be his last article. Can you?'

'It's a happy thought,' said Folly. 'Yes, I'll do it at once. I was about to sustain myself with a few *pâté* sandwiches and a glass of burgundy—but they can wait.'